DUST
AND
DECEIT

Book One of THE DUST TRILOGY

HEATHER HAYES

First soft back edition January 2020

Published by AH Digital FX Studios, INC 01/22/2020
AH Digital FX Studios, INC
10551 E. Ririe Hwy.
Idaho Falls, ID 83401
www.ahfx.net

ISBN: 978-1-945597-09-1

Library of Congress Control Number: 2020931569

Cover by Adam Hayes
Book Layout & Design by Adam Hayes

Paperback printed in United States of America

For Vicki

My supportive fan from the very beginning

Chapter 1

THE LOOK IN HIS EYE says he doesn't know why I have invaded his workspace. His thin, sun-tanned face twists in concentration as he asks, "How did you know where to find these shovels?"

The wind makes it hard to focus on his features. I push my blonde, windblown hair out of my face before I answer. "I read the sign on the back wall of the store."

The teenage worker's unruly dark-brown hair bounces as he scratches his head. "You're the first one to read that sign. It's been up for three weeks, and no one has come back here to get any of these shovels until now." He looks around at the

1

remaining gardening tools around us. "I keep hoping people will buy them so I won't have to find a place to store them until spring."

I think about what that says about the work ethic of the society I live in for a second. I want to make sure I didn't misunderstand. "The sign said buy one shovel get two free. Is that deal still good?"

The guy lifts a muscular arm to wipe the sweat off his forehead. Arms like that aren't very common these days. "Yep. I don't know what good three shovels will do you now that the harvest is done, but help yourself."

Not everyone who puts a shovel to the earth is growing something.

"My father sent me to get him a new shovel because his broke this morning. He isn't using it for gardening though..."

I can see the gears turning in the young man's head. "It's getting a bit late in the season to start building. We may get snow before the month is out." The guy shrugs and goes back to stacking bags of mulch in a storage shed.

A slight frown crosses my lips as I say to his back, "I know that. My dad sometimes does things out of season. He'll be thrilled that he gets three shovels instead of one. Thank you." He turns around briefly and nods as he picks up another bag of mulch. I pick the three shovels with the straightest handles out of the stack leaning against the wall of the hardware store and check the tips for sharpness. They could cut my finger if I'm not careful. Perfect.

I haul them through the back door of the store to pay for them inside. The clerk looks a lot like the teenage boy outside. I bet she's his mother. He's probably only a year or two older than me. I really wouldn't mind working side-by-side with someone who knows how to work up a sweat. "Ma'am, are you hiring by chance?"

The middle-age woman snorts. "No. My boy and I are barely keeping the doors open on our own. We can't afford to hire anyone right now. Try again in the spring."

"Okay. Thank you." As I pull the coins my dad sent with me out of my pocket, I look back at the sign on the wall of the store. It says, "End of Seeson Clerence, Buy One Wooden-handled Shuvel, Get Two Free. Located behind the store," in big red letters. I try to decide which is sadder, that I was the first person in three weeks to notice such a good deal, or that there are three spelling errors in this one sign.

As I leave the hardware store, I feel something soft wrap around my ankle in the breeze. It's a dirty-looking plastic sack. I kick it off irritably. There's always garbage blowing in the wind. It's so gross. My parents have taught me to pick up litter everywhere I go, even though no one else does, but I don't have a spare hand right now. It doesn't do any good anyway.

I look longingly down the vacant street at the largest building in our city, the library. It used to be a shining beacon

3

to those who lived here 100 years ago. Unfortunately, hardly anyone goes there now. As the sun sets, the large building looks like a decrepit mansion with only four out of hundreds of windows lit up. I would stop to pick up a book, but my hands are too full of shovels to get one now. I better get these back to my dad before he does something stupid.

The farther I walk, the heavier the shovels get. Only two more blocks to go. I am watching my feet instead of the road when a loud roar from an engine startles me. I jump out of the way before the town drunk, Vern Craigstaff, can bump into me with his beat-up old truck. "So sorry, girlie. I think I had one too many," he laughs out his open window. "Are you all right?"

I feel my racing heart start to slow down. "Yes. I'm fine. You really shouldn't drink and drive, Vern."

Vern wipes his long, straggly hair out of his face. "I know, I know. I have paid for more mailboxes than I can count. Heh, heh. I do know better. I'll stay home for the rest of the night, little missy. I'm so sorry. Have a nice night." I smile and wave as Vern pulls away, more carefully this time. He may have a drinking problem, but at least he is pleasant and has a conscience.

"Hey, Dandra!" a deep male voice calls out. I look around in the semi-darkness until I see my friend Conrad sitting on his fancy front porch swing a couple of houses down.

I'm happy for an excuse to set the heavy shovels down once I reach his huge house. "Hey, Conrad."

Conrad's dark eyes glower at the shovels in my hands. "It looks like you're enabling your dad in his—unhealthy obsession."

I force my eyes away from Conrad's black, perfectly-spiky hair. "Uh, well, Dad doesn't care what anyone else thinks, and he's determined to do it, so I'd rather help him than watch him hurt himself."

Conrad's tall, agile body leaps over his front steps and hefts the shovels onto his shoulder. I hope they don't snag his fancy silk shirt. His big brown eyes look at me curiously. "Why does he need three shovels? He can only use one at a time."

I sigh. "I only meant to get one, but they were on sale today. You know money is always tight, and these three will probably last him a year."

My friend looks at me with concern and lowers his voice. "You know that he'd get in trouble if a patrolman knew what he was up to."

I laugh as I start walking. If Conrad wants to talk, he'll have to carry my shovels and follow me. I flip around backwards to face him. "Do you know a single patrolman who is willing to get his lazy behind out of his car and actually investigate a random project like my dad's?"

Conrad's eyebrows come together. "Well, not in our town. They really should do something about Vern though. He almost hit you just now. I'd file a complaint if I were you." I shake my head and wave his comment off. He looks at me sternly. "I've seen some active patrolmen in other towns who crack down on crime and drunk driving."

I wrap my faded purple jacket around me as the wind picks up. It's always colder when I cross into the shadow of the country border wall.

I keep the shivering out of my voice when I say, "Vern doesn't drive farther than the bar and his house. I don't think he's a major threat to the community, and I really don't mind the patrolmen we have here. We don't need men in uniform up in our business all the time. Until the City of Tifton replaces the patrolmen we have, or the President of Layland sends his personal patrolmen, my dad's secret is safe."

Conrad shakes his head at me as I open the wooden gate to my front yard. I hope he doesn't notice that it could use a fresh coat of paint. Instead of going inside, we push our way through a slight gap in the thick, bushy hedge that blocks the view of our backyard from the street. The other side of the house has equally thick bushes with our old pickup truck parked in the middle of them. Gas is so expensive that we hardly ever drive it. Conrad hands me the shovels one at a time through the gap in the left-side hedge before he follows me through. A little branch scratches his face in the process. "I wish you would trim these back," he grumbles as he gingerly touches the scrape on his cheek.

I give him a sympathetic smile. "I know, but then my dad wouldn't have privacy back here." We drag the shovels across my enormous backyard to our old shed, which looks like it's leaning against the back fence. The single lightbulb hanging from the ceiling of the tool shed attracts flies better than it repels the darkness that is settling in fast. The giant sheet of plywood that is usually on the ground is propped against the wall, exposing an enormous hole in the ground.

Chapter 2

CONRAD AND I DUMP THE SHOVELS on the ground next to the hole. The sound startles my father, and his messy, salt-and-pepper hair pops out of the darkness. His blue eyes light up when he sees us. "Well, hello, Conrad! I haven't seen you in a few days."

My friend gives my dad half a smile. "Yeah, it's nice to see you too, Mr. Metty."

Dad's eyebrows crease. "How many times have I told you to call me, Gifford?"

"All the time, Mr. Metty—Gifford."

My dad shakes his head and smiles at my friend as he limps

up the ladder. We back up to give him room. He does a double take when he sees the shovels on the ground. "Wait, whoa. Where did you find money for three shovels, Dandra? As much as I'd like to have a couple of spares, we can't afford all these."

I am quick to reassure him. "There was an end-of-season clearance at the hardware store, so I got three for the price of one."

Relief washes over Dad's face as he brushes the dirt out of his graying hair. "Wow. Excellent. That's the kind of lucky break we need right now. Mother just found out that the Braxtons are switching to a different tutor starting next week. With me losing a class, that cuts our income in half."

I frown. "What do you mean? I thought the university was giving you an extra class to teach this semester."

Dad's face droops. "No, you misheard me. They aren't offering one of the classes I usually teach anymore, so I'm down one class."

Conrad shifts his feet uncomfortably in his brand-new shoes. "I think dinner is probably ready; I better get back home. I'll see you around, Dandra."

I smile at my friend. "Bye! Thanks for carrying the shovels!"

He grins back. "No problem."

As we watch my friend leave through the bushes, my father sighs. "I never thought I'd see the day that I'd be teaching only one class a semester."

I feel the breath leave my lungs. "You used to teach five or six a semester. This is ridiculous."

My dad looks at his hands as he picks the dirt out from under his fingernails. "Hardly anyone signs up for classes anymore. No one wants to learn. They just want an easy job that will put a simple roof over their heads and pay for their gaming. I'm lucky to have a class left at all. Most of the high-level professors at The University of Tifton have been laid off the past few years."

I look at the ragged edge of my pants and wonder if we'll be able to replace them any time soon. "So if you only have one class to teach and mom has just one student to tutor, how are we going to pay the bills?"

My dad's eyes fill with fire. "We'll figure out a way. Don't you worry about it and don't worry your mom and sister about it either. We paid off the house two years ago and it is very important that we stay here. We may have to sell a few things, but we will stay on this property. I picked this house twenty years ago because it is the closest anyone in our country can get to the border. Speaking of that, do you want to see how far the tunnel goes? I'm a good ten feet past the back fence. I'm almost to the border wall."

I grit my teeth and force the corners of my mouth up at my dad as I lower myself into the hole. He leads me into the tunnel he has been digging for ten years. The tunnel is about six feet tall by five feet wide with five feet of earth over my head. The curved top made it hard for my dad to brace and support this whole thing with straight pieces of wood. Luckily, my dad is the smartest guy I know, and with lots of engineering research, he made it work. My dad's hair brushes the ceiling as we walk. The wooden supports all along the walls of the tunnel make me nervous to use the old-fashioned oil lanterns that my dad has burning. But we do the best with what we have. I personally prefer using the two flashlights we own to light the way into the abyss. As I walk, I imagine where the backyard fence line probably ends and where no man's alley begins. I see a dull shovel with a broken handle on the ground next to a pile of dirt at the end of the tunnel. "Were you scratching dirt away with the broken shovel while I was gone? You were supposed to be relaxing."

Dad smiles at me sheepishly. "Yes. There isn't much build-up right now because I just sold a pickup load of dirt to Jim."

"What does he use the dirt for?"

"He still hasn't told me, and honestly, I don't want to know."

I shake my head at him. "Regardless, you promised not to dig until I got back with a new shovel."

My dad's eyes crinkle as he smiles at me. "You worry about me too much." We maneuver around a big wheelbarrow as we look at the dead end. My dad pats the dirt wall in front of us and beams at me. "One good thing about losing a class is that I'll have more time to finish the tunnel. I plan to be under the country boundary wall and into The United Cities within the next year."

I can't fake a smile anymore. "Dad, what if all of this backfires? We don't know much about The United Cities. They don't let people in or out of that country very often, and I've heard that they lock up all people with physical flaws and treat anyone who is less than perfect like garbage. My eyes wander to my dad's lame leg. "I don't want any part of that."

Dad pats my shoulder and leads me back to the opening, extinguishing the lanterns as we go. The sound of his voice ahead of me fills with emotion. "Dandra, I wish you could have seen the city when I was a boy. It was so clean and beautiful." Dad turns and looks at me as he leans against the ladder. "I was part of an inventing club and a book club before and during my high-level schooling. I loved meeting with people who wanted to talk about things that really matter. Our invention club never made anything more life-changing than a pig-pellet-making machine, but the meetings and the fairs in the park brought so many people together, and I got so many good ideas from those conversations."

"What happened?"

"Unfortunately, our invention club dwindled over the years. It got down to only two people. My buddy, Bob, kept coming over to work on our inventions only because he knew it meant so much to me. Once I finished my degree and got a teaching job, I felt like I had to focus on my students more than on my own hobbies, so that was the end of that."

"Did you give up the book club, too?"

A smile spreads over my dad's lips. "The book club was a once-a-month indulgence that I refused to quit because it was where I met your mother." He pauses to relish the thought. "She was so well-read that her book recommendations were always accepted for the next book of the month. We had more classes to teach than we had spots to fill our first few years of marriage. It was amazing—then the gaming district was built." Dad's shoulders droop as he sighs. "The focus of the city turned from enlightenment to entertainment. I never knew how much that shift of focus would change everything. Our book club stopped reading books. They wanted to meet at the gaming district instead. Our beautiful library, parks, and universities had fewer and fewer people until now they are..."

"Empty," I finish for him. His sadness is contagious. I wish I could live in a world with book clubs and active hobbies. "Couldn't you start an invention club or book club again? We could bring the good times back."

Dad smiles at me and shrugs. "I've tried. It's so hard to find people who care about anything except their own entertainment and comfort anymore." My dad pauses for a second. "Although—there is a new group of younger people who might be interested—except they are known lawbreakers, so, never mind." He shakes his head. "That's why I can't just sit here. Watching education rot in this country makes me sick to my core. We are some of the most educated people in this town, and yet we live like paupers. They shut down another room in the library last week, by the way. If anyone wants to see a map or an encyclopedia, they are out of luck."

My heart sinks. This is news to me. I looked something up in an encyclopedia at the library nine days ago. They must have shut that room down just after I was there. I try to remember the last time I traveled outside the city. It's been several years, and we try to experience the country more than anyone else I know. If gas wasn't so expensive, we'd be on a different mountaintop every month, I bet. Since people don't travel any farther than the gaming district anymore, they won't notice that the maps are gone.

He looks at me curiously. "Don't you need encyclopedias and maps for your homework? They should leave the room open for that."

"The low-level students like Everley might, but I rarely have homework, Dad. When the teachers assign it, I'm one of the few who turn it in. We do almost everything in class now."

Dad grasps my shoulders and looks into my eyes. "The dean of the university told me that a new senator has just been elected in The United Cities. He wants to free the flawed people who have been locked up over there. He wants to change how their whole country is run. I have a feeling he is going to make big changes for that country. I met a mayor from there years ago. He was disgusted with the filth and laziness of Layland. He said that the United Cities has clean streets and beautiful homes and that the universities and industries are still thriving over there. I can't just sit idly by like everyone else in Layland and watch our people turn into brainless oafs. Things have to be better on the other side of that wall. They just have to." His eyes burn with determination.

"I hope you're right," I sigh as I help my dad and his wobbly leg up the ladder. He doesn't realize that he isn't getting any younger. He is so sure that our country is falling apart and that the grass is greener on the other side of the fence. He may be right, but the closed border of our countries makes it impossible to know for sure. I would hate to see his face if he finds out that the country next door is no better.

Chapter 3

"DANDRA! WAKE UP! You promised to take me to the gaming district today," my little sister cries out as she flings open my bedroom curtains.

I cringe as the bright sun penetrates my eyelids. I pull my blanket over my face as I croak out, "I did?"

"Yes! You promised we could go on Saturday," Everley insists as she stomps her foot.

The conversation my dad and I had about money last night comes to mind. "Mom and Dad don't have any money to spare right now, sis."

"I know that. They never have money to spare, and they

don't approve of the gaming district either, but you promised we could use your birthday money from Grandma."

It all comes back to me. Everley came back from her best friend's 10th birthday party last Saturday crying because she was the only one at the party who didn't have money or a points card to stop at the gaming district on the way home. My parents tried to explain to her that food and clothing were more important to spend their money on and that gaming encourages sloth. She ran to her room and cried for an hour. I think gaming is a waste of time and money too, but I hate to see my little sister looking so sad. I promised her that I'd take her to the gaming district in a week and we could spend my birthday money on games. I kind of wish she had forgotten...

Everley stomps her foot again. "Get up, sleepyhead!"

I shouldn't have stayed up so late re-reading my favorite detective novel. "Okay, okay, go make me some oatmeal so we can leave sooner," I groan.

"Okay!" she agrees as she skips out of my room.

I sluggishly slide out of bed and get dressed into my best long-sleeved shirt. It hides how faded my pants are. I guess I'm not getting a shower this morning. I notice that my hair is getting darker at the roots as I pull it back into a ponytail. Mom taps my freckled nose with her finger as she walks into the lavatory.

"Where are you two off to?" she asks as she pulls out her make-up bag from the cabinet. I realize that we have the same blue eyes and long eyelashes as she applies mascara in the mirror.

I know she will be mad if I tell her the truth, so I make something up. "I'm taking Everley to a school activity."

Mother unscrews her practically-empty lipstick tube with a frown. "Why haven't I heard anything about it?"

I avoid her eyes. "Oh, they didn't send a notice home. It's a last-minute service project."

She purses her lips together and throws her lipstick tube in the garbage. She notices me watching her and puts on a smile. "That's surprising. What are they doing for this service project?"

"Uh, they are—cleaning up the litter on the low-level school grounds."

Mom's thin face lights up as she fluffs her short blonde hair in the mirror. "Really? I can't believe it! That's great. You two can show the rest of the community how it's done. Will you be back by lunch?"

"Uh, yeah. I think so. We may be a bit late though. Don't wait for us."

"Okay. I won't." The last of the hair spray hiccups on her head as I leave the lavatory.

As I eat my oatmeal, Everley's blue eyes watch me intently. It's so annoying. She twists her dark-brown hair around her finger like she is turning the cogs in my brain to get me moving faster. I spoon the last bite of my breakfast in my mouth. Her freckles squeeze together with a smile that could light up the town. "Let's go!"

I try to ignore the litter that blows against our legs as we walk to the other side of town. I shouldn't lie to my mom. Maybe we'll stop at the school and pick up trash after we go to the gaming district. As we approach Conrad's house, I stop and look at his front door. He would probably like to go with us. He loves gaming as much as every other boy in this town, but I've been trying to get him to cut back. If I ask him to join us, it may seem like I'm changing my stance on gaming. I better not risk it. We continue walking past Everley's litter-covered low-level school and the litter-covered park. The swings sway in the breeze, empty of occupants. This city feels like a ghost town sometimes—until we turn the corner. Bright lights and loud music greet us as we approach the gaming district. I keep the growl that wants to erupt out of my chest inside.

Chapter 4

EVERLEY JUMPS UP AND DOWN as the lights and sounds of the gaming district overpower us. We approach the huge doors to the vast building, and they open automatically. Inside, the red walls draw us in. My sister looks at me expectantly. "Which game should we start with?"

I slip my hand in my pocket and finger the five one-dollar coins that I find there. "I was thinking a game that takes a long time to play but doesn't use too many coins."

Everley's face drops. "Okay, fine. I guess we won't be playing any games of chance or skill."

"What does that leave?" I ask as I look around.

"Games of whimsy," Everley mutters through her frown.

A tall, squishy man in a red suit approaches us. "Hello, pretty ladies. Will you be playing with coins or winner points today?"

I definitely don't have any winner points, so I say, "Coins."

"An excellent choice," he says as he puts his point-card reader back in his suit pocket. "Do you know your way around, or would you like some assistance?"

I think he can see the discomfort in my eyes. "We—uh, could use some assistance."

"Perfect. If you'll just follow me." The gaming employee has more bounce in his step than I would expect for someone as soft and squishy as he is. He points to a vast expanse of brown tables on the right. "These are our games of chance. There is a minimum of $20 in coins or the equivalent in points to join these tables. More is always recommended, of course." He pauses momentarily until he sees me shake my head. "Very well. Straight ahead you can see the giant black screens and black tables that involve games of skill. Most beginners start on the left side consoles. Once you have a record of wins, you may be recruited to the team games that you see on the right."

There are only two teams here right now. They must be playing against each other. One team has six guys on it; the other team has four guys and two girls sitting side-by-side in short, black, cushy chairs. They are playing a game that requires them to shoot a person on the screen about every five seconds, but the thing in their hands doesn't look like a gun; it looks like a black box with handles. Everley gasps when she sees the digital guns shooting and the bloody digital bodies collapsing all around the screens in the room. I turn her head to look at me instead. These gamer teams look like they plan to stay here for a while. At least that's what the huge bags of food and drinks sitting next to them tell me.

"What are the yellow canisters for that are sitting by the gamers' feet?" I ask.

The worker turns a little bit red around the collar as he says, "They—um, they're for game teams who don't want to lose time going to the lavatory when they're in a major competition. Don't worry, the plastic shields around the top keep everyone from being exposed." If I thought he was turning red, I can just imagine how red I am right now. Or maybe I'm green. That is the most disgusting thing I have ever heard. The worker clears his throat. "These games of skill require a minimum starter fee of $10 in coins." I shudder and shake my head again. He frowns momentarily before he leads us to the left. "Over here we have games of whimsy. The most expensive ones are just ahead, starting at five dollars a game, and the least expensive ones are back toward the door at one dollar a game. Would you like to purchase a gaming card for a dollar to rack up winner points on?"

I finger the five dollars in coins in my pocket and decide that I'd rather give Everley five games instead of four games and a points card. "We'll start at the low-end games. Thank you so much for your assistance."

"Don't you want a points card?" he asks again as he pulls an orange card out of his pocket. "The more you win, the more you can keep playing for free."

I look at the orange card and its little window with twelve little zeros lined up in a row. "No, thank you," I say with conviction. I won't let this place keep me here a second longer than it has to. The employee looks at me like I have two heads before he walks away.

Everley leans toward me. "Did that guy say that gamers use those yellow canisters to..."

I shudder again. "You heard what he said. You can see why we stay away from this place. They are indulging lazy, disgusting behavior here, and I don't want to talk about it anymore. Play your games and let's get out of here."

Everley frowns at me. "How much do you actually have?"

"Five dollars, so pick the five games you want to play carefully."

She rolls her eyes at me as she looks over the seven games that cost a dollar to play. "I guess I'll just play the single-player ones." She sticks out her hand expectantly.

I give her a one-dollar coin and watch her mount a plastic-looking motorcycle. She is pretty cute as she swerves around turns and jumps over speed bumps. Before I know it, she's done and sticking her hand out for her next coin. She does a surprisingly good job on the shooting game, especially considering how much she cringed in the other room and the fact that she has never shot a weapon in her life. She stinks at the flying game but excels on the dancing game. Squares light up on the floor and she has to step on them before they go dark. She decides to do that one twice. When the lit-up dance floor goes dark, she sticks out her hand to me.

I pull out my empty pockets. "Sorry, sis. That's our last coin. Game over."

Everley's happy face crumples. "No! Are you serious? I was so close to beating the high score."

"Hey, I know you guys," a familiar deep voice says from behind me. Conrad raises his eyebrows as he approaches us. "You two are the last people I expected to see here today. I didn't think you approved of gaming, Dandra."

How did I know this would happen? I give him a flat look. "I don't. I was indulging my sister, but we were just leaving."

Conrad scoffs at me. "But Everley was about to beat the high score! Here, you can use some of my winning points for one more round." Conrad swipes his orange card through the dancing machine console. I roll my eyes as I watch points subtract from his card.

My sister beams like it's her birthday. "Thank you, Conrad." Everley is super focused as the dance floor lights up again. She somehow moves her feet to the right square before it lights up.

Conrad bumps me in the side with his elbow. "Wow, she's a natural at this." I give him a wary look before nodding in agreement. He smiles as he looks around the gaming district that seems to go on forever. "Be honest. This place isn't as bad as you thought, is it?"

It is bright in here, and many people seem to be excited, but knowing how much time and money they are spending here makes me sick. "Well, um..." I am saved from putting together a response that he won't like when the song Everley is dancing to increases in volume and extra lights start flashing. "What is going on?" I ask in alarm.

He nods at the scoreboard. "She just beat the high score. She's going to pay me back the points I spent on her." He pulls out his points card and watches the number in the window of the card go up. "And—she just passed it. Now I owe her another game."

I can't believe it. I just want to get her out of here. "I don't know how she can beat the high score when she's only played the game twice. Didn't you say you spent months trying to beat the high score of your favorite game?"

Conrad turns toward the back of the gaming district. "Yeah, well, the high score I was trying to beat was a game of skill on one of those giant screens. Everybody loves that game. This dancing game isn't very popular. Most games that make you work up a sweat aren't high demand, so the high score isn't really all that high, if you know what I mean."

I look around at the slow-moving people around me. "That figures."

When the lights and sound turn off Everley's game, she jumps down. "Thank you, Conrad."

"No, thank you! You racked up a bunch of winning points on my card when you beat the high score. You should play again!"

Everley squeals, "Yay! Thank you!"

The next thing you know, we'll be camped out in a chair and peeing in a bottle with the rest of these people. I clear my throat loudly. "Actually, we have to get back home for lunch. We better go."

Everley moans, "No, I don't want to go."

Conrad pulls a wrapped piece of candy out of his pocket and restores the smile to my sister's face when he hands it to her. "No problem. I'll walk you guys home."

When I turn to the front doors, I am amazed at the crowds of people pushing their way into the building. I grab Everley's hand so I don't lose her. We get pushed against a gaming machine and both of my feet get stepped on. "Ow." I grimace at Conrad and ask, "Why are there so many people here now?"

He looks at the clock. It's just after noon. "It's gamer's morning. Most gamers stay up late and are just barely waking up now."

I notice that the people pushing past us are wiping the sleep from their eyes and are trying to flatten their messy hair

HEATHER HAYES

with their fingers. "Ugh, they look like zombies." Conrad takes a look around and laughs in agreement. I'm glad Conrad still showers and combs his hair. I raise my voice to be heard above the crowd. "What do your parents do for their jobs here, again?"

"Dad is part-owner, and mom is an accountant. They run the numbers on what it takes to run this place and how much it brings in."

I watch the zombie-like people pulling out their orange winner's point cards and swiping them in every game as far as the eye can see. "Huh. Does this place bring in a lot of money if most of these people are using points to play?"

Conrad looks at me like I'm missing the obvious. "Oh, yeah. This place makes tons of money. Most of these people are in the Mega-Monthly Points Club. They pay a monthly fee for a set amount of points plus they get double the points that coin-payers earn."

"How much does the club cost?"

"I'm not exactly sure because I get it for free since my parents work here, but I think it's like $100 a month." He smiles at me like that's a good thing. I am not going to tell him that we walked in here with only $5 between us. "Hey, Dandra, I couldn't help noticing that your dad was worried that you spent too much on shovels. If you're looking for a job, maybe my parents could get us both jobs here." His eyes light up. "That could be fun."

I watch the lady next to me sipping a soda with blank eyes

28

as she plays a digital smash-everything-up game. It makes me uncomfortable. "Uh, no thanks. I'd rather work at the library. Let's get out of here."

There are so many people pouring in the automatic doors that I gravitate toward the smaller stationary doors to the side. Conrad holds a door open for Everley and me as his eyebrows form a V-shape. "You'd rather work in the library? You're kidding. That creepy old place?"

I feel myself tense defensively. "Yeah. That creepy old place." A man with a blank stare wearing a sloppy t-shirt and pajama pants almost walks into me. I give Conrad a pointed stare. "It has less zombies than this place."

Conrad snorts as we cross the street. "I'll admit, the gamers that come in during gamer's morning look like they could use haircuts and showers, but I think that calling them zombies is going too far."

Everley pipes in. "Yeah, Dandra. I was gaming, and I'm not a zombie."

I smile at her indignation. "You're right. You're not a zombie. I should watch what I say."

Conrad hands Everley another piece of candy, which she takes gratefully. He looks at me thoughtfully for a second. "You know, Dandra, if you embraced gaming, you could make a lot of money, like my brother does, unlocking things in games for people who are willing to pay."

I roll my eyes. "How much does he make?"

"I don't know for sure, but I know it's at least double what the guys in the red suits make. And—if you joined a gaming team, you could win team battles and competitions to make money."

"Have you made any money doing that?"

"Yeah! My team took fourth and made $50 in coins each last month at the Skull Crusher Clash."

I grab his shoulders and make him face me. "Yet each of you have been paying $100 a month to get good enough to join a team and practice for this clash thing. I'm sorry, but that is not making money; that's spending money."

"I am not as hard-core as most of the gamers around here. I know people who have quit their jobs and make good money at the weekend competitions."

I let his shoulders go. "If you say so." I shake my head. "Believe it or not, I'm not interested in any job that involves the gaming district. I want a job that makes the world a better place for everyone."

Conrad bumps me in the side. "You know that working in the library will affect hardly anyone, right?"

I scowl as I look at the tall, weathered building in the distance. "If I could give the library a facelift, maybe more people would come inside to get books."

The doubt in Conrad's eyes is hard to ignore. "I don't know about that." My frown makes him backpedal. "But if anyone can get people to use the library again, it's definitely you."

My cheeks suddenly feel warm. That was a nice thing to say. The low-level school grounds are just ahead of us, and I'm not going home feeling like a liar. "Want to help us pick up the litter at the school, Conrad?"

I can't tell if the sound coming out of him is a scoff or a laugh. He looks into my eyes and says, "You have a really strange sense of fun, Dandra." He puts his arm around my shoulders and says, "But I like you, weirdness and all. Let's do this."

Chapter 5

THE SCHOOL GROUNDS look 100% better when we leave them, but before we are even around the corner, I see a couple of kids drop candy wrappers on the grass. I growl as we head home. The job of picking up litter is never done. Is it even worth the effort?

We are so late for lunch that our plain ham sandwiches are hard and crusty on their plates. Conrad takes one look at what we're having and says he is supposed to eat with his parents and brother, and leaves. While I choke down my dry sandwich, I watch my mother count the dollar coins in her purse and stack them into little towers on the bills that need paid. The coins run out before two of the bills get a stack placed on them. I smile and pretend not to notice the deep crease between my mother's eyes. It is definitely time to get a job.

I TRY NOT TO FROWN AS I APPROACH the gigantic building that I love. The sign above the door hasn't been fixed since vandals ripped a couple of chipped black letters off. It says, "LI RA Y." I force a smile as I pull with all my might to open the rusty front door. The smell of dust and rot assaults my nose as I walk into the enormous atrium. The sight of so many books, even if they're dusty, still sends happy chills through my body. Sometimes I wonder which came first, the library, or Agatha, the librarian. She nods at me from behind her circular desk as I put the detective novel that I finished last night into the book return.

As I open my mouth to speak, she turns around to dig into a box of books. Her gray bun bobbles as she says, "No, no one has turned anything in from the detective section, but an old man returned a mystery novel yesterday that has been hiding under his bed for 20 years. You may like it. It's on the second floor...."

I don't even wait to hear what the title is. "Perfect! I'll go get it." I run up the creaky staircase to the second floor and take a left past a few doors until I get to the room filled with mysteries and detective stories. The door is only slightly less rusty and creaky than the front door. I flip the light switch on, but the light is so coated in dust and grime that it doesn't improve my vision in here much. I can see why Conrad calls this place creepy, but to me, this particular book room is a paradise. My eyes scan the floor-to-ceiling dusty books until I find a single brown-covered book free from dust. This has to be the book Agatha was talking about. As I pull it out from the shelf, the neighboring books rain dusty particles onto my hand. Ew. I quickly shake them off. I really wish Agatha would dust up here once in a while. I know this isn't a popular section, but still...

I start reading as I head back to the stairs. I'm so engrossed in the introduction that I don't notice that I've passed the stairs and am making the full loop of the second floor. Agatha looks up from her desk at me and shakes her head as I walk the circle of the outer landing. A mouse startles me from my book as it crosses my path to a boarded-up door and scurries underneath it. Double ew. The plaque on the door that the mouse went under says "Encyclopedia and Map Room." My dad was right, they've closed it. The knowledge-filled pages of those books are going to become nothing but mouse nests. The thought turns my stomach.

I shut my book and pay enough attention to slowly slink down the staircase this time. The ancient librarian raises her eyebrows at me as I approach her. "Agatha, please tell me that the encyclopedia and map room is not permanently shut down."

I wonder how much of the wispy gray bun on the librarian's head is actually gray dust particles as she checks out my book. "I'm sorry, darling. You and your father are the only ones who have used that room in the last year. When the mayor came last week to see how we could consolidate expenses, he said that we couldn't afford to heat a room that isn't being used."

Anger flares inside of me. "But I use it! I can think of ten things I'd like to look up right now!"

"I know, darling, but it's just like the room of histories and the room of nonfiction and the room of science. Your family were the only ones who used them, and they had to be shut down to conserve money."

I feel my heart drop to my feet as I look at the boarded-up doors around the atrium—two on the first floor, two on the second floor, and two on the third floor. The front door of the library suddenly screeches open to bring me out of my depressed stupor. A pimply teenage boy rushes past us, up the stairs to the second floor. He takes an immediate right. Agatha's chair squawks as she rolls to the side where a damaged book is awaiting her attention. "I'm sure he's off to the game cheats room or the comic book room. They are the only two rooms I don't worry about closing down this year."

I am positively sick. I pull out a chair by one of the many

empty tables around the atrium and plop down; my book is all but forgotten in my hand. I've been thinking about money ever since my dad told me about our financial troubles, and I was determined to ask Agatha for a job at the library today. But, if they are shutting down all the rooms I love, they probably can't afford to give me one.

"What's eating you, kid?" Agatha asks as she adjusts her bejeweled spectacles on her wrinkled nose.

My shoulders slump without my permission. "I—I came today wanting to ask for a job, but I can tell that you're not hiring."

Agatha grunts as she leans back in her chair. "That's right. Zelma and I are the only librarians left, and we don't get as many hours as we'd like."

The dust in the air makes me sneeze. I rub my nose in irritation. "I understand." I feel another sneeze coming and it gives me an idea. "I just thought that you and Zelma could use a younger set of limbs to do the dusting and arranging on the upper floors, but I can see now that I was mistaken. *Achoo!*"

Agatha's eyes rise to the dust bunnies covering the chandelier high above her head. She unconsciously rubs her nose too. She taps her long fingernails on her desk before saying, "I may not have a shift to give you, but if you are willing to climb on ladders and stairs, maybe I could give you some of my wages for dusting all the hard-to-reach places in here."

I jump to my feet. "Really? That would be great!"

Agatha tries to look disinterested as she scoots in her rolling chair to a drawer of files. "When can you start?"

I would love to start right now, but I shouldn't look as desperate as I feel. "Tomorrow. I get out of school at 3:00; I will come straight here."

"Perfect." Agatha opens a thick folder entitled "Budget" and looks at the top paper through her spectacles. "I think there is a little bit of janitorial money I can use as well. Make sure to wear clothes that you don't mind getting dusty in."

I have very few nice clothes anymore. "Oh, I will! Thank you, Agatha. This means so much to me."

She scoots her chair to the other end of her desk. "I'm surprised there is a young'un willing to work a dirty job in this city anymore. The kid I hired two years ago quit after one day."

I think of all the times I've helped my dad dig his tunnel. "I don't mind dirty jobs."

Agatha nods. "Do you mind weird sounds? That's what made the kid I hired three years ago quit. We have more than our fair share of squeaks and squawks around here, but don't worry. I've worked in this library for forty years, and the sounds of this old building have never hurt me."

It's almost like the building responds to Agatha's statement when it gives a long, low creaking sound. I force a smile. "That's a—relief," I say as I leave the library that seems to get creepier by the second.

Chapter 6

AFTER SCHOOL I HURRY excitedly to the low-level school to make sure Everley walks home with her friends before heading to the library. Agatha has a large bucket of supplies waiting for me on her desk when I get there. I slide the mystery novel I brought home last night in the book return. Agatha raises her eyebrows at me. "I can't believe you finished that already." I smile and shrug in response. "You'll be too tired to read tonight; I guarantee it. Pull those gloves up to your elbows so you don't turn black. You can only use dry dusters on the books, but I would like you to use soap and water on the thick grime and polish on the wooden shelves and trims. All of the curtains and light fixtures will have to be washed with soap and water, too. Take all books off a shelf at a time to dust, then put them back. You'll need a ladder. There should be two on each floor. I'd like you to start on the third floor and work your way down. If you haven't quit by then, I'll have you tackle the attic and basement too."

I pull the rubber gloves up to my elbows obediently. "Okay. I can promise you that I won't quit."

Agatha looks at me over her glasses. "Mmmhmm."

I find Agatha's lack of confidence unnerving as I march up the two flights of stairs to my destination. I think I'll start in the outer hall and then tackle the specialized book rooms. I find an empty book cart near the top of the stairs. It will work nicely as a temporary holding place for books as I dust each shelf. It looks a little bit grimy, so I fill my bucket with hot water from the lavatory to scrub it with. My idea works great to some degree. I take all the books off one shelf and put them on the cart. I dust and polish the shelf, and then dust each book before returning it to its place. The book cart keeps getting grimy again between shelves, but a simple wipe down remedies that. My arms get heavier and heavier as I circle the third-floor landing. I force myself to ignore the pain. I can collapse at home once I finish this outer ring.

Two hours in, Agatha calls up to me from her desk, "Are you ready to quit yet?"

I stop what I'm doing for a second and lean over the railing. "Nope. I'm doing great up here."

She leans all the way back in her chair and looks up at me. "Glad to hear it. You're faster than I thought you'd be." I smile at her and give her a thumbs up sign before getting back to work.

Sadly, only one person joins me on the third floor during my four-hour shift. That person is a red-headed girl who looks about a year younger than me. She comes into the library with her mom but slips up to the third floor for a few minutes. I smile at her as I wipe down a shelf from the top of a ladder, but she does not smile back at me. I'm kind of used to unfriendly people, but usually I get a blank stare back. This girl is not a blank-eyed person. Her eyes are big and green and...defiant? I watch her as she locates a book from each floor to check out. Her mom only checks out one book for herself. They leave just as quietly as they came. A few teenage boys check out game cheats and comic books, but the library doesn't see anyone else but these few people.

When the grandfather clock on the main floor gongs seven times, Agatha stands up and stretches her back before calling to me. "It's time to go, Dandra. The library closes at 7:00. Come collect your money."

I happily dust the last four books on the book cart and shove them back on their shelf. I dump the dirty water from my bucket down the third-floor lavatory sink and wash my hands. I am completely exhausted. I only have one more shelf of books on the outer ring of the third floor to dust. I can get it done next time before I start on the book rooms up here. My hands thank me for the warm soapy suds that I'm caressing into them. What a day.

As I leave the lavatory and pack up my supplies, I admire how nice the shelves look. I may have a long way to go, but I'm proud of the work I've done so far.

Agatha hands me a stack of coins as she leaves her circular desk. A quick count reveals that she's paying me the minimum wage required by Layland law. I wish it was more, but that's okay. I'm making one of my favorite places a cleaner, less-creepy place to be. I'm sure Mom and Dad will be happy to buy food with these coins.

Agatha grins when I place a newly-dusted book on the counter to check out. "Will you be back tomorrow, Dandra? Or have you had enough already?"

I take the book back and answer as energetically as I can, "I'll be back. I almost have the third-floor hallway done. I can't wait to see this whole place done."

"Well, good. I'll see you tomorrow then."

As I put my backpack on and follow a waddling Agatha out the door, I swear I hear something behind me creak as I exit the front door. "Did you hear that, Agatha?"

"It's just the building saying goodbye to us. You'll get used to it."

"Oh." I convince myself that the second creak I hear is a second goodbye from the building as well.

Chapter 7

CONRAD'S DEEP VOICE BRINGS ME BACK to the present. "Hey, Dandra. Wake up!"

I raise my head off my desk quickly, before Mr. Henry, my history teacher, sees me. It doesn't stop him from asking me a question.

"Dandra, what do you think is the most important educational amendment of the last 200 years in Layland?"

I straighten my back and answer confidently, "That's easy. The 'Library in Every City Amendment' is definitely the most important educational amendment we've had. Tifton built the second-largest library in the country because of that amendment."

"Yeah, and now it's the second-largest eye-sore in the country," a boy named Philip says to thunderous giggles from the rest of the class.

Mr. Henry pauses to think about what I said. "That's an interesting opinion. Does anyone else have an opinion on what the greatest educational amendment has been?" His question is met with silence and blank stares. He calls on a girl named Molly, but she doesn't know how to say anything except, "Um," and, "I don't know."

Conrad's voice whispers loudly to me again, "What's wrong with you? You never sleep in class."

I whisper back, "I stayed up late reading, and I think I wore myself out cleaning at the library last night. I had to climb up and down ladd—" the bell interrupts my story. I quickly shove my book and notebook into my backpack and follow Conrad out the door.

Conrad mumbles something as we leave, but all I see is the red-headed girl that I saw in the library yesterday walk past me looking straight ahead. My eyes follow her to her classroom, which happens to be beside my next classroom. How have I never noticed her before? "Hey, are you even listening to me?" Conrad asks.

I force myself to look at him. "Uh, sorry. What were you saying?"

"I asked what you thought about the educational amendment that is being proposed. If it passes, we would be done with middle-level school after this year. I kind of like the idea of being done with school by age 16 instead of 18."

I yank my backpack off my arm. "I think that is the stupidest thing you've ever said."

Conrad looks hurt. "You can disagree with me without being rude."

I feel bad for hurting his feelings. I let Molly walk in front of me and into our next class before I respond. "I'm sorry. I just can't imagine even more teachers out of work and our classmates even more clueless than they are now." My eyes point in the direction Molly walked.

Conrad takes my elbow. "But think about it. Most of the jobs in the city don't require more than what we know now. Why not quit wasting time and get to work?"

I come to a complete stop and reclaim my arm. "Did you really just say that staying in middle-level school is wasting time?"

Conrad's cheeks turn red. "Hey, you were the one asleep in class just now."

I run my hands through my stringy blonde hair, painfully aware that I didn't take much time on it this morning. "I don't usually do that. When is the vote on this amendment?"

Conrad takes a comb out of his pocket and hands it to me. "Two months from now."

Who keeps a comb in their pocket? I take it despite my shock. "Huh. We'll talk about this later." I slip into my next classroom before he can argue with me. After this class is lunch, and I fully intend to talk to the red-headed girl.

Mrs. Jones, my English teacher, divides us into groups to talk about an essay she had us read about national pride. I have plenty to say on the subject, but a boy in my group named Baldwin doesn't let me get a word in edgewise during our discussion. "There should be more free classes offered at the middle and high-level schools for those who want to better themselves."

I glower at him. "That sounds great except the professors won't make any money to live on that way, and no one is signing up for classes anymore regardless of what they cost."

Baldwin shakes his head. "That's only because the classes cost too much, Dandra."

Why couldn't I get grouped with the boys who only have things to say about their gaming teams and competitions? Or people like Molly, who don't have any opinions about anything? I'm so irritated with Baldwin and his list of problems with our country that I'm relieved when the bell rings for lunch.

I race out the door to find the red-headed girl. Her quiet and mysterious air helps her slip through the crowded hallway like a ghost, but I am more determined to talk to her than she is to sneak away. I grab the sandwich and apple I have stashed in my locker and follow her to—the school library. It's a tiny room with six shelves of books and three tables that hardly anyone uses. The skeletal librarian has her back to me as she eats her garlic-drenched salad at her desk. The red-headed girl is sitting at a table by herself with a book and a sandwich. I approach her table and pull out a chair. "Do you mind if I sit here?"

She looks at me distrustfully and whispers, "Sure." Her frown isn't very reassuring. She looks back at her book.

"I'm Dandra. What's your name?"

She halts before taking a bite of sandwich. Without looking at me she says, "I'm Charlisa." She takes a bite, looks briefly at a boy, who I'm pretty sure is in one of my classes, as he comes in and sits at a neighboring table, then continues to look at her book.

I situate myself at the table and take a bite of apple. This girl isn't very friendly. I wonder how I can get her to open up. She likes to read and visits libraries, which is rare. I bet we have more in common than either of us know. "I've never heard your name before. I know a Charlotte and a Lisa, but you're the first Charlisa I've met."

She looks up from her book long enough to give me a fake smile and say, "That's nice."

I refuse to be poisoned. "So, I just got a job at the city library. I'm cleaning all the dust and cobwebs off everything." Charlisa looks up long enough to nod at me but does nothing more. "I saw you there yesterday with your mom." Charlisa nods again. There is a hardness to her features. "I love to read.

My father is a professor, and my mother is a tutor." Charlisa looks at my frayed pants and patched backpack before she nods this time. "It doesn't seem like anyone else around here likes to read anymore. That's why I was so happy to see you at the library yesterday. What are you reading?"

Charlisa sets her book down and glares at me. "I don't know what you're trying to do, but it isn't going to work. What I read is my business—not yours. I don't know what you think you know about me, but I can guarantee you that you're wrong. I don't like answering questions, and I want to be left alone." She shoves her book and sandwich into her backpack and leaves without looking back. The boy at the next table over packs up his stuff and leaves too. What did I do?

Chapter 8

I AM STILL DUMB-FOUNDED when I get to the city library after school. I wasn't mean to Charlisa. Why was she so defensive? Agatha has the bucket of cleaning supplies for me again as I enter the building. "Let me know if you need anything, Dandra."

"Okay, I will." I say absentmindedly as I walk up to the third floor. I get the last shelf in the hallway dusted and polished first, and then I start on the room of how-to books. I am washing the glass from the light fixture in my bucket of soapy water when Baldwin from my English group bursts in.

"Oh, hey, Dandra. What are you doing here?"

I look pointedly at the bucket of dirty water in front of me like he is the biggest idiot in the world. "I work here."

Baldwin laughs as he starts reading titles. "I highly doubt that. They are shutting this place down. I bet the doors will be permanently closed in a year."

I feel my earlier irritation at him from class grow hotter. "You don't know that. Stop acting like such a know-it-all. Cities should have libraries. Besides, this temporary job could become permanent if it brings more people in."

His hands are scanning books quickly and efficiently down the shelves. "This job of yours is more temporary than you think."

He is irritating me from the top of his shaggy brown hair to the bottoms of his scruffy green tennis shoes. My voice hides none of my feelings. "What are you looking for?" I ask irritably. "I want to help you get out of here—so I can clean."

He raises his eyebrows at me for half a second. "Fine. I am looking for a book about how to fix radios."

I drop my soapy rag into the bucket and wipe my wet hands on my shirt. "I'm pretty sure all books about electronics are on the shelf to the left side of the door." I walk to the shelf and pull out a few dusty volumes before I find one about radios. "Are you talking about one-way radios or two-way radios?"

He seems surprised that I know the difference. "Two-way radios," he says as he takes the book from me. "This is exactly what we need. Thank you."

"Who's we?" I ask.

His eyes close off. "Oh, no one. See you in class," he says as he walks out the door.

He purposely didn't answer my question. I should have demanded an answer, but I tend to avoid confrontation as much as possible. I'm just glad to have him out of my space.

Chapter 9

I GET THE HOW-TO BOOK ROOM DONE and I'm almost done with the room of romance novels when I remember that my parents are making Metty soup for dinner tonight. My stomach growls in anticipation. It's a family recipe that takes beef and many vegetables to make, so we only have it about once a month. My father said he'd pick up the ingredients after work today and that we'd make it a weekly tradition while I'm working. I think it is his way of accepting some of my wages for the good of the family. I smile as I polish the shelf in front of me until it gleams. I wish my stomach would quiet down, but maybe I'm hearing—something else. I swear I hear something—

scraping coming from the inside of the wall. I set the stack of books that I was putting back on their shelf on my book cart instead and press my ear to the back of the shelf. *Scritch, scratch, plunk.* I am not a jumpy kind of girl, but I'm not imagining that.

I burst out of the book room and down the stairs to Agatha. "Agatha—I just heard a scraping sound in the walls of the romance novel room."

She leans back in her chair and raises her eyebrows at me. "Honey, I told you this old building has a lot of strange noises that goes with it. It is probably mice or rats climbing the inside of the walls."

"I—I don't think a rat made that sound. It sounded almost metal to me."

"Oh, come now. I've worked here for 40 years. I've heard rats make some pretty crazy sounds in these walls. I'll put out some rat traps for you. Will that make you feel better?"

Not really, but I guess it's better than nothing. "Uh, yes. Thank you."

"It's almost closing time anyway. Just finish the shelf you're on, and then start cleaning up for the night."

"Okay." I trudge up the stairs to the third floor and pretend not to hear the metal scraping sound as I put the romance novels back on their shelf.

As I leave the building with Agatha, I hear creaking noises again, but I know it will do no good to mention them to her.

IT TAKES A WEEK TO FINISH the book rooms on the third floor. I am incredibly proud of how it all looks. This whole building is going to look just as good as the third floor in a month. I start on the mystery and detective story room on the second floor because it's my favorite. I feel kind of bad as I enter the room. Agatha was right. I've been so tired since starting this job that I haven't read much. Oh well, I'm sacrificing some personal time for the greater good.

If I had a washing machine, I would wash all the curtains in the whole building together, but I don't, so I wash each room's curtains in my bucket of soapy water as I go along. When I have the mystery room's curtains hanging back up, I notice a shelf with no dust on it. Who has been reading all these Steadmans?

The answer becomes clear when Charlisa bursts in and takes a Steadman mystery off the shelf without saying a word to me. She can't avoid me forever. "Hi, Charlisa. Are those any good?"

She turns around in surprise and says, "They're okay."

"I think I'll take one home then."

"Suit yourself."

I should leave her alone, but I long for a friend who likes to read, so I say, "I would like to be your friend, Charlisa."

"I have all the friends I—" she suddenly turns her head

towards a scratching sound coming from the wall. I'm thrilled to see that I'm not the only person who hears it.

I approach the scratchy wall and press my ear against the bookshelf. "What do you think that sound is? I hear it all the time in the walls."

Charlisa looks angrier than she usually does. "It's— probably mice. You—should tell the librarian about it."

"I don't think Zelma cares..."

She yells at me, "Quickly!"

I frown as I straighten up. "Okay, okay. You don't have to yell."

I walk down the stairs to the librarian's desk and tell Zelma about the scratching sound in the walls. She laughs at me and says, "Don't tell me this is the first time you've heard a mouse scratching around this library."

"No, I see and hear mice all the time, but—"

"I have to tell you the story about the giant mouse nest I found on the third floor a couple of years ago...." Zelma's story fades off in my ears as I watch Charlisa leaving the mystery and detective book room. She has the same book I saw her with earlier, but I swear she didn't have the envelope that she's sliding into her pocket.

I stare her down as she walks down the stairs and hands Zelma the Steadman mystery to check out. I clear my throat. "Charlisa, did you need some time to decide on that same book?"

She refuses to meet my gaze. "Um, yeah. I like this series so much, it's hard to decide sometimes."

"Mmhmm."

She takes her book and heads to the door. "I'll see you at school, Dandra."

I'm too chicken to confront her. "Yeah. See you."

Chapter 10

THE METTY SOUP WE HAVE FOR DINNER is absolutely delicious. Everyone, including Everley, has seconds. When I've finished my second bowl, I push back from the table, but I don't get up.

My dad starts stacking the dirty dishes. "I'll wash if you dry."

I smile at him. "Deal."

Mom helps Everley with her homework at the table after we clear it off. My Dad makes sure the temperature of the water is warm, but not hot, before sticking his hands in the sink. He elbows me gently. "How do you like your job, Dandra?"

I shrug. "I like it. I'm exhausted after each shift, but it's worth it. I love the way the library shelves look when they are dust-free."

Dad smiles at me. "I've noticed the difference. I didn't sneeze even once when I was on the third floor yesterday morning." I smile proudly as he continues, "It is looking so much better that I may try to hold a staff meeting in the atrium when you have it all clean. Once the other professors see how nice things look, they'll hopefully send more students there."

I swap my wet kitchen towel for a dry one. "That would be great. Thanks, Dad." I take a dripping-wet bowl from him and slowly dry it with my kitchen towel. "Do you know of any groups that study two-way radios around here?"

Dad looks at me curiously. "Two-way radios? No. There haven't been classes on those since I was a young man. The only communication our country is focused on is regular telephones and communication between gamers."

"Oh. That's too bad." I imagine Baldwin reading the book I gave him. "I didn't know that gamers could communicate with each other."

Dad frowns and shakes his head. "There is an old device called the GameForever that people can play from home that connects with the gaming district."

"Huh. Why do so many people still go to the gaming district if they can hook up to the GameForever at home?"

"It doesn't work very well. As I understand it, the

GameForever is quite expensive yet slow and glitchy. People get a better gaming experience if they go to the actual gaming district."

That gets me thinking. "You'd think that gamers would appreciate study and education in order to improve their at-home gaming experience."

Dad smirks. "Yeah, you'd think so. But it's like I've always said, gaming dulls the potential of the brain." He scrubs a big pot with vigor. "Actually, now that you mention it, I'm hearing rumors about a new gaming device that will be available soon called the GameCom."

I wrack my brain for mention of that name but come up empty. "I've never heard of it." I look at my dad sideways. "There was a boy in the library the other day who seemed like he was part of a group trying to set up two-way radios again."

My dad looks at me in disbelief. "I'd be thrilled if there was a group into that, but I doubt it. I usually hear about things like that."

I roll my eyes. "Dad, anyone can check out a book at the library and learn something. You won't always know."

Dad sighs. "I hope that is still happening."

I imagine Baldwin reading how-to books in his room all night and Charlisa secretly learning something from her note. "I wish it was easier to find people to study with."

Dad's eyes look sorry for me. "Actually, now that you mention it, I know of a new group of youth who have no money for classes or books, so they steal books from the university and then teach each other. If I could get them to stop stealing and just learn from library books, maybe you could study with them."

I think of how little the high-level school is paying my dad these days. Those kids aren't making things any easier for us. "Great, so the only people my age who want to learn are also thieves?"

Dad pulls the plug out of the drain and watches the dirty water disappear. "Uh, yeah, maybe."

Chapter 11

WE HAVE A TEST IN ENGLISH CLASS, so I can't talk openly to Baldwin, but I think he may have a study group going on that my dad doesn't know about. As soon as the bell rings, I corner him before he can leave the room. "So, how is that radio book I helped you find working out?"

He looks at me with annoyance as he pulls on his oversized jacket. "It's pretty good. We're figuring things out."

I lean in. "Who's we again?"

He takes a step back. "Ah, uh, I just mean me. I'm figuring things out."

A loud crash makes us turn to a pudgy kid named Garry

who is shoving a million loose things into his backpack. He apologizes as he wrangles stray books and treats on his desk next to the door. He accidentally leaves a candy bar at his desk as he struggles out of his seat and out the door. Baldwin slips the candy bar up his sleeve as we walk past.

I'm not blind, and I'm not impressed. I would normally keep quiet, but I find the courage to ask him, "Baldwin, are you a thief?"

He keeps the hand with the candy bar hidden behind him as he answers dismissively, "Everyone is a thief in one way or another." And then he walks away without another word, and I just let him.

AS I CLEAN SHELVES IN THE LIBRARY, I wonder if Baldwin has stolen any books from here. He may have stolen the book about radios, for all I know. I will make a habit of following him to the check-out desk if I see him again. If he has stolen books from the university, I should alert my dad and the city patrolmen—well, if I have the guts. I'm glad he wants to learn, but stealing while learning gives education a bad name. Ah! I wish that terrible scratching sound would stop for once.

The walk home from the library is cold and so windy that I zip my purple jacket all the way up. My stomach growls as I get closer to home. When I turn the corner, the flashing lights of two patrolmen and one medical pod blind my eyes. What is going on? I see potatoes, carrots, and onions all over the ground surrounding a broken bicycle. When I see a package of beef bits sitting in a puddle of blood, the world falls out from under me. That bicycle is my dad's. These vegetables and this beef are for my weekly Metty soup.

I don't know how I end up on the ground, but I see spikey black hair to my right and a patrolman to my left. Their lips are moving, but I hear nothing.

Chapter 12

"DANDRA, DANDRA, you have to stand up. They're trying to clear the road." Conrad's words finally reach my ears, but they still aren't reaching my brain. "Stand up, Dandra. I'll take you home. There is a patrolman there ready to explain everything to you."

I feel myself stand up, though I don't know how it happens. I see a sheet covering a tall figure in the emergency pod before they shut the door. I hear bits and pieces of conversation and random noises, but they don't register with me as I walk with Conrad to my house, where there are more patrol cars lighting up the street like a Christmas tree.

My mother and sister are waiting for me with open arms and tear-stained faces when I walk in the door. I can't believe any of this is real. "What happened?" I whisper.

A tall, hefty patrolman steps forward and removes his hat. "An hour ago, a drunk driver hit your father, Gifford Metty, on his bicycle on Oak Street. The driver drove away, but your friend, Conrad here, saw it happen and wrote down the license plate number. After a thorough search of the city, we've found the vehicle and have taken the suspect to the detainment center." I wish with all my heart that the next words won't come out of his mouth. "Unfortunately, Gifford Metty died at the scene of the accident. I'm sorry."

There it is.

How can I ever unhear those words? How can I ever be whole again? I feel myself dropping again, but Conrad is there to direct me to the couch. Everley falls on my lap, crying. I hold her, but I can't speak. I don't know how to comfort her when I have nothing to give. Mother sits down next to us and wraps my sister and me in her arms. She cries with us for a while, but when the head patrolman clears his throat, she stands up and makes arrangements with him.

I don't know how long it takes before she sends them on their way. I'm not even sure what my name is anymore. I'm glad my mom has words for these people because I don't. After they leave, she breaks down into sobs and says she'll be in her room for a while.

Conrad sits next to me on the couch and gently rubs my back as I cry with my sister. I don't know what happens next, but the world goes dark. When I finally come to myself, it's morning, Conrad is gone, and Everley and I are waking up on the couch. Waking up to a world without Dad.

Chapter 13

THE DAYS COME AND GO. The funeral is a blur.
I know all of our family, friends, and neighbors cry with us. I
know it's the cheapest and simplest funeral we can come up
with. We have to borrow some money from Grandma to even
do this much. I know my mom cries when Conrad's family
donates lots of meat for the luncheon and flowers for his
graveside service. I know that the man I see in the coffin does
not look like the man who always loved me and smiled at me
with sparkling eyes. I know I run away when my dad's coffin is
lowered into the ground. I know Conrad follows me and holds
my hand like he has through most of this week.

I haven't gone to school or work since I collapsed on the street that horrible night. I wonder if someone told Agatha why. I sure didn't. It isn't until the funeral luncheon is over, and I hear my uncle say that he is going to find anything that will fetch a price from our shed that I wake up to my new reality. We are not just poor anymore. We are destitute. Not only that, but people are about to find out my dad's secret.

I jump off the couch and run to catch up with my uncle in the backyard. I pull his arm to stop him. "No."

He looks at me like I'm a baby kitten that needs protection. "What's a matter, Dandra? I'm just trying to find you guys some grocery money for the next month."

I physically place myself in front of the shed door and spread my arms. "No."

My uncle puts his hands on my shoulders and tries to pull me away. "I can't leave here knowing you have nothing in your mom's purse. Just let me sell a few tools to ease my conscience."

I don't know why I feel so strongly about my dad's secret, but I start yelling at my uncle. "No, Uncle Jack! If we need the money, we will sell his tools ourselves!"

He seems surprised at my resilience as he tugs on my arms. "I just don't think a bunch of women will know what they're worth. Let me help you!"

He doesn't look ready to give in. I stop fighting him and place a hand on his chest. "You wait here." I slip inside the shed and pull out Dad's two saws, closing the doors behind me.

"Here. You can sell these two, but that's it. We use the other tools, and I know how to sell them if we need to."

Jack stares at me. "You are a stubborn young woman, Dandra. I hope you don't make things worse than they already are for your mom," he says as he shakes his head and walks away with the saws.

I drop to the ground in front of the shed doors and rest my head against them.

"That's the most life I've seen in you all week," I hear a familiar, deep voice say. Conrad drops down next to me on the ground in his fancy Sunday clothes and takes my hand. "You know that you don't have to keep his secret anymore, right?"

I let go of his hand and look him in the eye. "Conrad, I know I don't have to, but I want to."

He loosens the long black tie around his neck. "I don't understand that. His ideas were a strain on you. You don't have to feel that anymore."

I feel a tear run down my cheek. "I don't know exactly how I feel about his ideas at this moment, but they are not something I want everyone else's opinion about right now."

Conrad's eyes reveal some kind of emotion that I don't understand—regret, maybe? He fakes a smile. "Um, okay, fair enough."

I feel like things are happening around me, but I haven't taken them in until now. I need to know what I've missed. "Conrad, who was the drunk driver who killed my dad?"

His eyes look sad as he rubs my hand. He pauses for an unnaturally long time. "I've talked about this in front of you several times, but I guess you weren't—listening. It was—Vern Craigstaff."

I feel my jaw drop. The news shouldn't surprise me since he almost hit me in his old truck not too long ago, but it does. "I can't believe it."

Conrad smacks the dirt off his black dress pants forcefully. "I'm sure he didn't mean to. Drunks don't know what they're doing half the time."

I remember Vern apologizing to me and asking if I was okay after he almost hit me. "I can't believe he just hit him and drove away."

Conrad shifts on the ground uncomfortably. "His truck and license plate number were unmistakable."

I imagine what Vern looks like in his old truck. "He is usually so kind..."

Conrad picks up a stick and chucks it across the yard. "They found your dad's blood on his dented bumper."

I'm not a person prone to anger, but I feel the ugly emotion building in my veins. I feel like I should confront Vern if I ever want to feel normal again. I pick up a stick and throw it even farther than Conrad's in my anger. "I'm—I'm going to the detainment center to tell him that his stupid choices have ruined my life."

Conrad scratches his head irritably. "There is no hurry,

Dandra. He's not going anywhere, and you just—buried your father. You need time to mourn." I feel tears building in my eyes. They must be from sadness. There's no such thing as tears of anger, right? Conrad is right; Vern isn't going anywhere. How does he know exactly what I need to hear?

I lean closer to him. "Conrad?"

"Yes?"

"Thank you."

His brown eyes look unsure. "For what?"

I squeeze his hand. "For being here for me."

The unknown emotion surfaces in his eyes again. "Any time." His hand tightens around mine, and he guides my head to his shoulder.

Chapter 14

"DANDRA, WAKE UP. You have to go to school today," my mother's voice insists.

I feel like my body is broken and can't move. "What? No. I don't want to."

My mother opens the blinds in my room despite my protest. "Dandra, you have missed ten days of school. If you miss any more, I'm afraid you won't catch up before the end of term."

I roll away from her. "Who cares? They want to cut off school at my grade anyway."

She raises her voice. "Dandra! Sit up!"

I never hear my mother raise her voice. I am still registering shock as I reluctantly obey her and sit up.

My mom sits next to me on the bed and takes my hand. "Your father would not want to hear you say that. If you loved him, you will show him what your brain means to you. You will get out of bed, take a shower, and walk to your middle-level school with an attitude to learn. Do you hear me?"

I nod my head even though I just want to stay home and feel sorry for myself.

"There will be a hot egg and hash browns waiting for you on the table in twenty minutes." She pauses and presses the wrinkles in her dress down with her hand. "I start my new job at the bank today."

I see the apprehension in her tired face. She is so much stronger than I am. "You'll do great, Mom."

She shakes her head. "I'm feeling out of sorts, too. Help me get us back on a schedule, okay?"

I hope I can do half as well as she is. "Okay, Mom."

She forces the corners of her mouth up. "You don't have to go back to work today, but I would really like it if you went back by tomorrow. We have to make our first payment for dad's funeral to Grandma in two weeks, and we need to pay the utilities. I hate to say it, but we'll both have to work to make ends meet."

My eyebrows lower as I take the truth in. "I can't believe Grandma didn't give us more time."

Mom pushes a loose piece of hair behind my ear. "Honey, she gave us everything she had. She really couldn't afford a funeral right now either. We have to pay her back, or she won't eat either."

"Oh." I had no idea. What a sweet grandma I have.

"If the library can't keep you on for long, you'll have to find something else. I'm sorry, honey."

I find some strength when I see the regret in my mother's eyes. "I—I will keep myself employed, Mom. I'll even go to work today. Don't worry. We—we can do this."

My mom gives me a tight hug and a kiss on the forehead before she walks out the door.

Chapter 15

I FEEL SURPRISINGLY OKAY as I walk Everley to her low-level school. I savor her hug a little bit more than I usually do when I drop her off. But then a block later, I see the blood spot on the road. I stutter step around it as I start to feel faint, but Conrad is there to put his arm around me and get me the rest of the way to school.

I had no idea how many people knew who I was until this moment. No less than 30 people have told me that they are sorry for my loss today. One of these people is know-it-all Baldwin during English class.

He looks almost tearful when he says, "Hey, Dandra. I'm

so sorry about your dad. He was a great man. He knew what mattered, and he had insightful things to say about—many subjects."

I wonder what that means. I force my head up. "Really? Like what?"

Baldwin scratches the back of his head which needs a haircut. "Like how this country is going to the dogs. People don't learn more than what a simple laborer and a gamer needs to know anymore." Dirk and another boy next to us are animatedly trying to recruit Lawrence to their gaming team. It cements Baldwin's point.

I roll my eyes. "Are you trying to say that you aren't a gamer like every other person in this room?"

"That's exactly what I'm saying. I'm too poor to be a gamer, and I have other hobbies that keep me busy." I notice his worn-out green sneakers again.

I feel my old, curious self awaken. I don't want to be weird or pushy, but I am almost positive that Baldwin in connected to the group my dad told me about before he died. I find some courage as I squirm in my shoes. "So what hobbies do you have? Besides two-way radios?"

Baldwin looks me in the eyes for the first time ever. His eyes are a dark chocolatey brown. They are a little darker than his brown, shaggy hair. It's like we're finally seeing each other as people instead of things. He opens his mouth yet is stumped on what to say for the first time that I can remember. "After everything you've been through lately, I can't believe you remember that."

"Why wouldn't I remember that?"

He smirks. "Dirk and Molly couldn't remember the title of the book we've been reading all year long in yesterday's discussion."

Mrs. Jones frowns at us as she clears her throat. "Keep your groups' discussion on the lack of farmers in the country, please. If you don't know what else to say, skim-read the article again."

I lower my voice. "Of course, I remember. You didn't answer my question though. What else do you do with your free time?" I hesitate before adding, "Does it have anything to do with my dad?"

Baldwin smiles at the teacher and then lowers his voice to me. "I—I read a lot. I'm trying to learn things that are disappearing from our world. Your dad has been to a few of the same—lectures as I have."

"What kind of things are disappearing?"

"All kinds of things."

"Are you hoping to change the attitudes of our country? Do you want to be a politician?"

He shakes his head and grins. "No, originally I wanted to, but like I said, I'm poor. I've given up on that. Now I just want to..."

The bell for lunch interrupts us. Baldwin packs up his

things and nods at me before he leaves. I feel...disappointed. I'm sure he was about to spill a big secret. I sigh and rub my temples. I shouldn't care; I have enough things at home to worry about. I'm at least proud of myself for speaking up.

Chapter 16

WHEN I GET TO THE CITY LIBRARY after school, Agatha's stern demeanor cracks a little because of her grief over me. Her voice is deep and low when she says, "I will miss your father, Dandra. He was my absolute favorite patron. Our city will suffer from his loss forever."

I feel closer to Agatha than I ever have. "I know. Thank you. I will do my best to keep his ideas alive in me."

She wipes a tear off her cheek. "Of course, you will."

I twist my hands together as I form the words I need to say. "I need to talk to you very seriously about this job, Agatha.

If you can't afford to pay me, I need to know, because I can't go without a job anymore. We need the money."

Agatha nods. "I understand, darling. I wish I could pay you forever, but I can probably only pay you until my next meeting with the mayor. That's in a few weeks. I'm afraid he's going to reduce my wages again and shut down more rooms."

I let the reality of that statement sink in. "Okay—I'll keep my eyes open for something else starting in a few weeks. Thank you for allowing me this time, even though it is a temporary thing, Agatha."

Agatha reaches out and pats my hand. "It has been my pleasure. I've enjoyed the dust-free shelves, and I think our patrons have too. They keep asking when the first floor will be done. We can hope that your cleaning will bring in more people and impress the mayor. Then he won't shut anything else down."

I force an unconvincing smile. "We'll hope," I say as I take my cleaning supplies and head up to the second floor.

The good thing about grief is that mindless, repetitive motions can be soothing. My body is happy to be out of bed and doing something, even though my mind is still foggy. I don't stop cleaning to talk to patrons, I don't pause to listen to the scratching in the walls, I just get into a rhythm of shelf cleaning until the entire second floor is dust-free. As I pass the boarded-up encyclopedia room on my way down to the first floor, I hear something. I swear I hear a book fall off a shelf in there. Did

Agatha leave books on the edge of the shelves before locking the room? That seems so weird. I'm not in the mood to talk to Agatha about mice again, so I just take my cleaning supplies down the stairs and collect my money.

"Are you ready to start the first floor tomorrow?" she asks.

I nod. "Yeah. It felt good to do something productive today."

She claps her hands excitedly. "Our patrons will be thrilled. You get a good night's sleep now. You deserve it more than anyone."

I swallow the frog in my throat. "Yeah. I'll try."

Agatha holds up one of my favorite detective novels. "Do you want to check out a book to take your mind off things?"

The frog finds its way back to my throat somehow. "No. Not today."

MY MOTHER CRIES THROUGH DINNER. She burned the potatoes, but we don't have any more to replace them, so we just eat them. I tell my mom that they aren't so bad, and I hand over my wages. Looking at the tiny stack of coins makes her cry harder.

When she regains control of herself, she says, "I'm so sorry, girls. I should have been paying better attention to dinner. I just had a hard first day at the bank, and my mind wouldn't stop going over what I should have done differently. This will get easier, I promise."

Everley clears her throat as bravely as she can. "I'll make dinner tomorrow. Will that help? You two have to work, and I get home earliest. I know how to make toast and eggs."

Mother takes Everley's hand as she breaks into tears again. "That would be wonderful, sweetie. Thank you."

Everley wraps her arms around Mom, and I wrap my arms around them both. I don't have any tears left to cry. I'm just mad that we've been forced into this situation.

After the dishes are done, I walk out to the shed and take my frustrations out on the tunnel walls.

Chapter 17

I DON'T KNOW WHAT COMES OVER ME, but after I drop Everley off at school, I skip class and walk to the detainment center. I have never skipped a class for anything but sickness or...death before.

The receptionist is not convinced that I should talk to the man who killed my father. When my words don't convince her, my tears do. She leads me into a white-walled room with a chair in front of an interior window. There is a metal slatted hole under the glass. I wait patiently for Vern Craigstaff to be brought to the other side of the window. When he shows up, he looks miserable. Forced sobriety doesn't agree with him.

I feel almost—sorry for him, but this new anger sensation is stronger. He killed my father.

I lean toward the metal slatted hole in the wall. I'm hurt and angry, but the words don't come easily as I look into the miserable man's eyes. "Why—why did you have to get drunk and run over my father?" I croak as a tear rolls down my cheek.

His eyes look crazy as he blurts out, "I didn't do it! I was framed!"

Fire races through my veins. "His blood was on your dented bumper. Just admit it," I spit out.

Vern laughs humorlessly. "That bumper has been dented and bloodstained for years. I hit a deer a long time ago."

I don't like the doubt that creeps into my mind. I push my hair behind my ears. "The blood they found was fresh and—it was my dad's."

Vern shakes his head. "The only driving I did that day was from my house to the dump, where I work, to the bar on 12th Street, and back home again. I didn't even drive down Oak Street where he died."

I stand up and glare at my dad's murderer. "My friend, Conrad, lives on Oak Street, and he saw you do it, Vern. I know you can't bring my dad back. I just—want to hear you apologize for—ruining my life." I choke back a sob before it escapes my lips.

Vern sets his free shaking hand on his knee to steady it. "Listen, I always admit when I've hit a mailbox or a cat, and I pay what I can to replace it. I would gladly do the same for your family, young lady, but I didn't do it. I came home from the bar and collapsed on the couch. The patrolmen showed up a while later and hauled me here. No one believes me when I say I'm innocent."

I feel so conflicted as I look at Vern's face. Part of me really wants to believe him, but the evidence says he's lying. Conrad says he's lying. "Vern, are you calling my best friend, Conrad, a liar?"

Vern looks me in the eye and says, "Yes, young lady. I am."

Chapter 18

I WALK BACK TO SCHOOL not knowing what to believe. If Vern didn't hit my dad, his blood wouldn't have been on his truck.

I slip into English right before the bell rings. We get divided into groups again. I'm surprised when Baldwin trades Kyle seats so he can be in my group. He lets the other members of the group take control of the discussion for once. He leans over to me and asks, "What's wrong? You look terrible. Did you come back to school too soon?"

I frown as I imagine how terrible I look and shake my head. "I just went to see my dad's killer. He says he didn't do it."

Baldwin raises his eyebrows and nods. "Don't all criminals say that?"

I feel stupid for saying anything. "Yeah, probably."

Baldwin looks around the room cautiously and lowers his voice. "Actually, I know Vern. He is as drunk as drunks get, but he's always been completely honest with me."

I look at him curiously. "How do you know him?"

Baldwin waits for the other kids in our group to turn toward the teacher before answering. "My dad introduced me to him. I met him at his work one day, and he, uh, let me crash at his house once when I had nowhere else to go."

I scoff as I imagine the scene unfolding. "Why would you choose to stay with him over your friends?"

"Uh, my friends were actually—it's a long story, but Vern told me that he'd be out late drinking, so not to be alarmed when he came in drunk that night."

I feel my body tense angrily. "Everybody knows that much about him."

Baldwin lowers his voice. "He came in even later than he planned because he hit a mailbox on his way home. He rushed inside and dug through all his change cans to pay for the mailbox. I thought that was pretty honorable."

I remember Vern's concern for me when he almost hit me; he could have driven away. "Yeah, I always thought he was surprisingly honorable—until he hit my dad."

"Just remember that there are two sides to every story. Unfortunately, your dad can't tell you his side."

A sob escapes my lips without my permission. I stand up and leave the class without an explanation. Luckily, the teacher just lets me go.

Chapter 19

AT LUNCH, CONRAD HOLDS MY HAND, but I don't like how it feels; or maybe I don't like how I feel.

He has no idea what is bothering me. "Where were you this morning? You missed class."

I don't look at him. "Yeah, I didn't feel so great this morning, but I'm here now."

Conrad rubs my hand with his thumb gently. "Do you want to talk about it?"

"Not yet."

He pushes a piece of my hair behind my ear. "Do you want

to come over after work tonight, so we can talk and maybe have some ice cream?"

I lean away from him. I'm not sure how to put my feelings into words, but I do need to talk to him. "Okay. I'll be there."

ZELMA WORRIES ABOUT ME when I clean all of the first floor's outer bookshelves in one shift without stopping. "You are going to wear yourself out, young lady. You should sit down and relax with me for a bit."

I don't slow down. My brain needs the fast, repetitive motion. "No thanks. I'm on a roll today. I just want to keep going."

She raises her eyebrows and shakes her head. "Fine. Suit yourself."

The second and third floors have bookshelves flat against the walls on their outer rings. The first floor has an actual floor under the whole thing, so besides the bookshelves against the wall, there are five times as many bookshelves that make another ring. I dust and polish all of the outer shelves like a mad woman as I think about what to say to Conrad tonight.

I collapse into a chair when I'm done. Zelma wakes me out of my stupor when she plunks a stack of coins on the table in front of me. It's time to go. It's time to interrogate my best friend without him knowing it. I really don't want Conrad to be a liar.

MY STOMACH RUMBLES as I ring Conrad's doorbell. A heavenly smell wafts in the open window. I think they had steak for dinner tonight. I should have gone home for dinner before I came here. I hope my stomach doesn't embarrass me while we talk. At least he promised me ice cream.

Conrad smiles as he opens the door. "Come in. Have you eaten yet? We're having steak and potatoes, if you're interested."

I don't know if I've heard a better offer in my life. "I came straight from work, so I haven't eaten yet."

Conrad's mom, Jerika, hears me as she comes down the hall. "Perfect, you can eat with us." She looks at my dirty, straggly work clothes and grimaces as she says, "I'll show you to the lavatory so you can freshen up."

I wish washing my hands will change how I look, but it won't. "Thank you. I hope I'm not imposing."

Jerika waves me off. "Oh, not at all. Conrad said that his older brother, Milo, would be home for dinner tonight, but it turns out that he had to work late, so we have an extra plate."

Conrad looks awfully pleased with himself. I wonder if he planned this. "What a lucky accident for me, I guess."

"Yes—a lucky accident," Jerika says as she smiles and directs me into the lavatory. "I'm so sorry about your father. I hope the flowers, hams, and roasts we sent helped out a little."

I pause at the door of the lavatory. I should have thanked her at the funeral, but I have been so out of it. "Oh, yes. They were perfect. The funeral wouldn't have been the same without them. Thank you. I'm sure my mother will send you a note to thank you from all of us."

Jerika Chesterton raises her eyebrows. "I'm sure she will. Wash up, and I'll see you in the dining room."

I'm happy when she finally leaves me alone for a minute. I don't know what it is, but Conrad's mom is giving off a strange vibe today. I don't like it. It's like she wants me to feel inferior or indebted to her or something. I feel that way already without her pointing it out.

Conrad and his father, Zane, stand up when I enter the dining room. I feel so shabby compared to them in their casual yet fancy clothes. Conrad pulls out a chair for me, and Zane slaps a huge steak onto my plate. It looks delicious. I hope I can finish it. I never eat this much meat in one sitting.

Zane smiles at me as he cuts into his own half-finished steak. "I hope you came hungry, Dandra. That's a Milo-sized steak."

"I'll try my best to have a Milo-sized appetite," I say as Jerika places a loaded baked potato on my plate beside the steak.

Zane lifts his glass of wine and says, "Atta girl. I wouldn't want Conrad's girlfriend to leave our table hungry."

I look at Conrad to see if he will correct his father, but he doesn't seem to see anything wrong with what his father said. I clear my throat, "I'm not—we're actually best friends."

"Is that what they call it these days?" Zane says as he leans toward Jerika and laughs.

I feel my cheeks burn as I keep my eyes on my steak. I steal a glance at Conrad, but he won't look at me. Dinner is incredibly uncomfortable. I smile, nod, and do my best to finish my steak, but I can't quite do it. Conrad and Jerika don't finish their steaks either, so I don't feel too bad. When I help Jerika clear the table, I'm shocked when the unfinished meat goes into the garbage can. Surely someone would like to eat the leftovers for lunch tomorrow. At least at my house, we would.

Jerika tries to get out the ice cream, but Conrad insists that we're too full for dessert right now. I'm thankful to be excused from the kitchen and on my way up the stairs with my friend.

He takes me into his room and shuts the door. I sit in his desk chair and sigh. I really don't want to talk about my dad's death yet. Luckily, there is a book and a weird, metal, light-up, circular thing on his desk to distract me. "What is this thing?"

Conrad hovers in front of the desk for a minute but then sits down on his bed. "Oh, it's a gaming device. It probably won't interest you."

I pick up the book and scan the back cover. "So, this must be the manual for it. It's good to know that you read once in a while, even if it's only to improve your gaming."

For some reason he's frowning at me from his bed. Maybe the sarcasm that made me smile was too harsh. He pats the bed next to him. "Don't you want to sit on the bed next to me?"

I pick up the metal device and examine it. "Naw, I'm fine here."

Conrad's face droops. "Please, it would mean a lot to me."

Oh. Okay. How can I refuse my best friend when he puts it like that? I set the metal device down and join him on the bed bumping him with my shoulder. "What was up with your dad thinking I'm your girlfriend?"

Conrad looks at me like I have two heads. "Why do you think you're not my girlfriend?" An uncomfortable silence follows.

I see pain in Conrad's face as I stumble on my words. "I—we've always been good friends. Best friends, even."

He looks at me like I'm missing something obvious. His words are hard to hear. "But when your dad died, you clung to me. You were always holding my hand or hugging my side." He takes my hand as if to prove his point.

I resist the urge to pull away. "Conrad, I—I was in pain. I am in pain. The worst pain imaginable. I thought you were—supporting me."

"I was. I just thought—we became more than that."

Oh, no. What have I done? Do I like him more than a friend? His sad face tears me up inside. Does that mean I like him that way? I don't know. Maybe? No, he might have lied to me. I can't believe I have to make a decision right now of all times. I came here to have a very different conversation than this.

I look into my best friend's beautiful dark eyes and hate myself as I say, "Conrad, I am in a really messed-up place right now. I like you more than anyone, but I don't want to call us boyfriend and girlfriend while I'm—lost."

Conrad's face crumples. "I was afraid you'd say that. Everyone else in school thinks we're together—everyone but you."

Is he serious? Nobody at school asks me about us. But—I guess I haven't been there much lately, and I don't talk to very many people in general. "Why do you want me for your girlfriend anyway? You are rich and handsome. Every girl in school wants to be your girlfriend. Why do you want me?"

Conrad's eyes light up a little. "So, you think I'm handsome."

I'm sure he can feel the heat coming off my face. "I—yeah. You are."

Conrad smiles and squeezes my hand. "I like hearing you say that. You are such a mystery sometimes."

I squeeze his hand back. "I love being friends with you. I just don't know if I'm girlfriend material."

Conrad sighs. "I feel like everyone else likes me for all the wrong reasons. They want to get in with my parents. You—I don't know if you even like my parents. You hardly ever come inside to talk to them." He laughs and kisses my hand. "I know that you like me for me."

I flinch a little bit as a fire starts on the spot where his lips touched my hand. "Conrad, I do like you for you. It's nice to have someone with an actual opinion to talk to." His hopeful eyes aren't thinking beyond—right now. "But, I'm poor, and my parents are eccentric. They teach me things that no one else believes in anymore. I'm a weirdo."

Conrad laughs and leans in. "Yes, you are a weirdo, but I like your kind of weirdness. Your bright blue eyes and cute freckles are hard to get out of my head—" I don't get a chance to explain my weirdness more because Conrad silences my lips with a kiss.

I don't know what I thought my first kiss would be like, but this is not what I expected. It's kind of nice and familiar in a way, but it's all his doing. Shouldn't I feel like an active participant? Shouldn't my heart skip a beat? When he pulls away, I watch his eyes open slowly. What do I say now? He says he can't get me out of his head. That's—sort of nice.

He watches my mouth as I say, "Conrad, thank you—for everything. Can you give me time to process all of this? I'm thrilled—yet confused. I need some time."

He pushes a piece of hair behind my ear. "Okay, I can wait. Just don't push me away while you think."

I try to make my head clear. "Okay. Thank you."

He bumps my side. "So why weren't you at school this morning? I missed you."

Oh yeah. That. "I—I went to see Vern Craigstaff at the detainment center." This is not how I wanted to start this conversation.

Conrad's demeanor goes from adoration to tension. "Why did you go see him?"

I rub my hands on my thighs nervously. "He says he didn't hit my dad. He says he was framed."

Conrads's eyes go hard and blank at the same time. "Guilty people always lie to get out of trouble."

"Conrad, did you see him do it? Did Vern run over my dad?" So much for being sneaky.

His attention is suddenly on a loose piece of thread on the bedspread. "I was right there in my yard, Dandra."

"Ice cream!" Jerika sings out as she bursts into the room. "Sorry for rushing in, I just had to make sure you two love birds weren't doing any hanky panky."

I curl in toward myself and away from Conrad.

"Mom, you are so embarrassing," Conrad groans as he stands up to take the two bowls of ice cream from his mother. I think my opportunity to get information from him is gone.

Chapter 20

I CRY MYSELF TO SLEEP. My mom pokes her head in to see if I'm all right. I don't want to tell her about Conrad, so I just tell her that I miss Dad. Which I do. I always do. She surprises me with an idea.

"Dandra, come with me. I'll take you where I go when I want to feel close to him." Mom puts a robe around me and takes me outside to the shed. Of course. This is Dad's special place. When I get to the bottom of the ladder, Mom lights a lantern and we walk to the end of the tunnel. The top part of the back wall is dug out a few feet thanks to my anger yesterday, but the bottom part is just waiting for someone to finish it.

I do feel closer to him in here for some reason. I touch the nail holes in the support beams and acknowledge that this is the work of his hands. I pick up a clod of dirt in my hand and crumble it. As I watch the dirt fall through my fingers, I ask, "Mom, do you think Dad was crazy?"

She laughs and touches my cheek gently. "He was either crazy or a genius."

"So, which one is it?"

She laughs and frowns at the same time. "I swap back and forth all the time. Now that I work at the bank and see what people spend their money on, I think more and more that he was a genius."

"Why?"

"We are lost in this country. Children are not nourished physically or mentally, but they have a lifetime supply of mindless entertainment."

I think of my small circle of friends and hope for a better future than that. "It could change, Mom."

"Maybe, but I doubt it. There is a new gaming device that hit the market today. It goes around the wrist like a huge watch, and it is extremely expensive. I watched 30 different people clean out their accounts to buy one today. They have nothing left for food or clothing or housing, but they have constant gaming, so that's all that matters."

That description sparks something in my memory. "I wonder if that is what I saw on Conrad's desk tonight."

Mom rolls her eyes. "Probably. His parents are the ones who paid to develop it."

That makes sense. "Dad wouldn't have liked it."

She huffs, "No, he didn't. He heard about its development and actively spoke out against it at the university and at a meeting with the mayor."

I look at my mom in surprise. "Huh, I didn't know that."

"Your dad was an active and involved person, Dandra. Not even I know everything that he was involved with, but this tunnel was his biggest priority."

I look around at the brown walls surrounding us. "Do you think this tunnel will ever get finished?"

She raises her eyebrows. "Only if we do it."

I kick the nearby wheelbarrow. "Yeah, right."

Mom looks at me in all seriousness. "If I start digging for an hour a night, will you help me?"

I shake my head. "We don't have time, and we'll break our backs."

Mom picks up a shovel. "Yeah, we might. But we might come out the other side in a place better than you can even imagine."

Great, she is just as crazy as Dad was. "I'll consider it, but I still think it's a little bit ridiculous."

Mom looks at me cautiously before speaking. "Dandra, your father had a lot of—unpopular ideas. I think he knew his life was in danger. That's why he started digging this tunnel.

He knew we would need to get out one day. I just wish he had finished it a little bit earlier, so he could escape with us."

I roll my eyes. "He died in an accident; you can't plan for that."

Mom pauses before speaking. "That's what the patrolmen wrote in their report, but I have a hard time believing it."

I look at her intently. "Really?"

Mom's eyes fill with alarm. "Yes. Please don't repeat what I'm about to say. Your father had enemies."

"Who?"

"Anyone who wants to keep the people of our country ignorant."

Chapter 21

CONRAD WAVES AT ME the next day at school, but he doesn't sit by me in class or at lunch. That's really weird. Is this him pushing me away, or me pushing him? I don't know, but I'm afraid I'm going to get in trouble for it. At lunch I sit next to a boy in scruffy clothes that I'm pretty sure is in my math class. He looks like he needs a friend as much as I do. "Hey, I'm Dandra. What's your name again?"

The boy looks up from his single piece of bread and an apple that I'm almost positive came off the school's apple tree out front because I picked one too. He keeps a straight face as he says, "I'm Adamar. You're Professor Metty's daughter."

My head snaps up as I unwrap my dry ham sandwich. "How do—did you know my dad?"

Adamar shrugs. "I've listened in on a few of his lectures before."

I'm surprised when Charlisa, the red-headed ghost, sits down next to Adamar and gives me half a smile. She has an incredibly big lunch for such a petite girl. I'm even more surprised when she speaks to me. "Dandra, did you break up with your boyfriend, by chance?"

I force down a chunk of dry sandwich. "I don't have a boyfriend."

"Huh, that would explain why he looks so down today." She points across the room to Conrad, who is surrounded by people who are talking to him as he ignores them. He doesn't look like he got any sleep last night.

I am such a horrible person. I turn back to Charlisa and pull the dry crust off my sandwich. "How long have you thought he was my boyfriend?"

Charlisa gives half of her sandwich and one of her cookies to Adamar. I swear her hard demeanor cracks for the shortest second. "At least a year."

Adamar shoves the cookie in his mouth in one bite.

I slide the pieces of crust away from me. "Why did you think that?"

She raises one eyebrow at me. "You're always together."

I realize that she's right. "I guess we are. I am such an idiot."

Charlisa takes a long drink from her water bottle. "Did you give him the friend talk yesterday?"

I break off a small piece of sandwich. "Yeah, sort of."

Adamar pipes in, "That's rough." He takes the pile of crust in front of me and swallows it in one gulp.

Charlisa bumps him with her hip and bats her eyes at him. I guess she's okay with his disgusting eating habits.

Why did I think that this guy needed a friend? Charlisa is like a completely different person around him. "Are you two a thing?"

Adamar smiles at Charlisa, and she smiles back. She leans toward me. "Yes, but not in public."

As I'm processing that, Baldwin sits down on Adamar's other side. "Hey, Adamar. Did you figure out the cabling problem we were struggling with yesterday?"

I frown at Adamar. "Are you Baldwin's friend too?"

Adamar laughs and gives Baldwin a high five. "Yeah, we're practically brothers." I take in the scruffiness of clothes and shoes of both boys and realize that my clothes aren't much better. Is Adamar's poorness why Charlisa wants to keep their relationship a secret? She's not rich, but she's not scruffy either. I have a lot to learn about relationships.

I don't understand why Charlisa and Baldwin, who used to be so cold toward me, all of a sudden want to sit by me and talk like we've been friends forever. "Has something changed, Charlisa? The last time I tried to have lunch with you—"

Charlisa swats Adamar's hand off her knee as someone walks up behind me. She points upward with her eyes. "Dandra, I think Conrad wants to talk to you."

I turn around to see my glum friend staring at the people at my table. "Dandra, want to go for a walk before the bell rings?"

I hope he doesn't expect an answer about our relationship already. "Yeah, sure." I don't know what to expect as I shove my leftover food in my backpack. Conrad watches me with sad eyes as I stand up and wave at my new—friends. "See you guys around."

Charlisa and Adamar wave. Baldwin looks at me with concern. "Hang in there, Dandra. Hard times don't last forever."

"Yeah, thanks."

Conrad doesn't take my hand, but we head out the door side by side.

MY BEST FRIEND LOOKS UNHAPPIER than I've ever seen him as we walk to the parking lot. He turns to me and touches my hand. "Why are you pushing me away? You promised you wouldn't."

I take his hand. "I'm not. You were surrounded by people by the time I got to the lunchroom. I had to sit somewhere."

"Why did it have to be them?"

"I—it didn't have to be them. I just chose a table and sat there."

Conrad's eyes darken. "You know that they hate my family, right? They're anti-gamers."

I've never heard of anti-gamers. "I—I had no idea, actually, but it sounds like we would get along since I'm not into gaming either." A big piece of newspaper blows into me. I peel it off and crumble it up.

Conrad shakes his head. "No, you're not the same. You just like to do other things. They are part of an actual group that wants to tear down the gaming district and destroy gaming devices. They've cut the power to my dad's building twice. He had to send the patrolmen after them the last time. The patrolmen kicked them out of where they live.

My mouth twists in disbelief. "How can they do that? I highly doubt that their families allowed that to happen."

"Dandra, they don't have families. They're homeless."

Chapter 22

I CRY AS I DUST the first-floor book rooms after school. What is wrong with me? Have I just buried my head in the sand for so long that I don't know anything about anyone? Am I just so poor that I'm too consumed with my own survival to notice anyone else suffering? As I wipe a rag full of polish across an empty shelf, someone appears next to me out of nowhere. I scream and drop my rag on the floor.

Charlisa bends over and picks it up for me. "What is wrong with you, Dandra?"

I wipe the tears from my cheeks and take the rag from her. My voice is wobbly. "I feel like such an idiot. I didn't know

Conrad liked me, I didn't know you had a boyfriend, and—I didn't know you and your friends were homeless."

Charlisa laughs quietly as she starts scanning the dust-free shelves for books. "I'm not homeless."

I feel like a double-idiot now. "I'm so sorry. Conrad said you guys were anti-gamers, and that you were homeless."

She smiles at my discomfort. "Do you believe everything Conrad tells you?"

"No! We're friends, but we're very different, and we're actually struggling to know where we stand with each other."

"Dandra, because of who your father was, I kind of want to trust you, but I'm not sure if I can. Conrad is as gamer as they come and attached to your hip."

Is she saying that she is considering being my friend? "I'm sorry I believed him today. I just don't know much about these things. My parents are pretty old-fashioned. I've actually seen you with your mom. I should have realized that you're not a homeless anti-gamer."

Charlisa's green eyes stare at me for a moment as if sizing me up. "Oh, I am an anti-gamer, and most anti-gamers are homeless, but I live in a nice little house with my mother and father. She's not too happy about my circle of friends. I have to be sneaky to help out the cause."

Huh? I look at her curiously. "What's the cause?"

She lowers her voice and leans in toward me. "We're trying to get our country back—but if the educational amendment passes and Layland ends up a hopeless mess, we're going to get out."

"Wow, you sound like my dad."

Charlisa smiles and puts a hand on my shoulder. "I'll take that as a compliment." She looks around the room and exhales anxiously. "Yesterday our gang voted on whether to invite you to join us or not."

I start to sweat a little. "What did you decide?"

She smirks. "Will you join us?"

My heart bursts with excitement. I can't believe this is finally happening. "Yes! I've been waiting to find thinkers like you guys my whole life."

She squeezes my shoulder gently. "Even if it means losing Conrad Chesterton?"

What? I feel like I've been stabbed in the heart. Is she saying that I can only join the anti-gamers if I give up my best friend?

Before I have a chance to say anything, Charlisa's stern-faced mother bursts in the door. "You are taking forever, Charlisa. Let's go!"

Charlisa's face goes blank. "Sorry, Mom. I'm coming. I'll talk to you at school tomorrow, Dandra. Bye." She gives me a pointed look as she leaves.

I'm still in shock at what has been proposed to me. "Okay. See you then."

Chapter 23

AS I WALK OUT of the fourth book room on the first floor, I am surprised to see Conrad standing by the door. Agatha grins and winks at me as she hands me my pay. "He's a good-looking boy, and he's been waiting for you for the last twenty minutes."

I try to downplay her excitement. "Yeah, he's a good friend like that."

I gather my backpack and jacket while Conrad watches me. I notice as I approach him that he has the silly metal game thing around his arm. He takes my hand with his game-free hand as I approach the door. His eyes are red. "I had to take my dad to the shop to pick up his car. I told him I'd walk home with you."

I wish I felt happier. I'm happy that he thought of me, but sad that I kind of want to join a group of friends that won't accept him. How unfair is that? I would never put stipulations on friendship like that.

I cringe when the door creaks. He'll think that's creepy. I force a smile. "I'm exhausted, but it's nice to have someone to walk home with." I breathe in the cold city air, which is filled with delicious aromas. Of course, it makes my stomach rumble.

Conrad raises his eyebrows. "Do you want to stop and get some beefy patties on the way?"

I'm too hungry to refuse. "Sure. That sounds great."

It's just like it used to be, Conrad and I talking and enjoying each other's company as we eat, except he keeps looking at his wrist whenever his gaming thing makes a noise. It's moderately annoying, but it's when I look into his red-rimmed eyes that I know things will never be the same. As we turn on Oak Street, I see that his dad's car is safely back in their driveway, and then I see the blood spot. I stop walking and just look at it.

Conrad wraps his arm around me and keeps me moving. "You're almost home. Keep walking." I swear Conrad is almost as upset as I am.

I'm able to talk once I can't see the blood spot anymore. "It's so hard, Conrad. I miss him so much. He would know how to help me."

Conrad slows his pace. "What do you need help with? I want to help you. Does my GameCom make you uncomfortable? I can take it off."

I shake my head. I'm not thrilled that it keeps stealing his attention, but that's not what's bothering me most. "Tell me about the night he died. Did Vern Craigstaff do it?"

Conrad swallows as we approach my front gate. "I don't know how drunk he was, but he knew he hit your dad when he drove away. I—I had to do my part by telling the license plate number to the patrolmen." He pauses, truly upset at the memory.

I wrap my arms around him and hold him for a minute. "Thank you. Thank you for looking out for him and me."

Conrad kisses my forehead and turns to go. "I have to get back. It's late. See you tomorrow."

I reach for his hand, but he's already out of reach. "Thank you, Conrad. Bye."

Chapter 24

MY MOM WASN'T KIDDING about digging for a while each day. I was hoping that we could just relax for the rest of the night. "Girls, I'll be in the tunnel out back for the next hour if you need me," she says with a smile. She doesn't ask me to join her. Once I hear the door click, I feel guilty about not following her out there. Everley is busy drawing a map of Layland for school at the end of the table, so I just kiss her forehead and tell her that I'll be in the tunnel with Mom if she needs me.

Mom's shovel is hacking at the dirt with all her might when I get to the back of the tunnel. "Are you okay, Mom?"

"Yeah. I'm fine. This is just a good way to work out my frustrations."

"Bad day at work?"

She pauses mid-stride. "Sort of. I'm the newest person at the bank, but I'm doing the most work out of all the employees."

That comment makes me smile. At least she has confidence in herself. "How can that be if you don't even know how to do everything yet?"

Mom shakes her head. "It's those stupid GameComs. They are so distracting to all of the employees. Even the people who don't have one can't keep their eyes off everyone else's wrist."

I think about how distracting Conrad's was tonight. "Conrad wore his tonight. It was pretty annoying, but I haven't seen any at school or the library yet."

"They're too expensive for most kids your age to have, but it'll change. It'll play out just like your father said it would."

This is news to me. "What? Dad knew this would happen?"

"Yes, honey. He spent the last years of his life fighting against gaming as his classes emptied out. He knew that if people could keep their games on them at all times, then the desire to better themselves would cease."

I let that sink in as I chip out the last chunk of hard dirt from the half wall we are working on.

"Did Dad ever mention a group of people called anti-gamers?"

Mom stops for a drink of water. "Yes, he met with them a time or two. Why?"

"I didn't know they existed until today. The only people who have any brains at school are part of that group. They seem like the kind of friends that I would like to have. They're trying to recruit me."

She nods. "I'm sure your father would approve. It sounds like a good thing to me."

I feel my shoulders droop. "Yeah, it does seem great, except I can only join if I ditch Conrad. He and his family are not too crazy about anti-gamers."

"Oh." Mom nods like that is the understatement of the year. "That is why your dad didn't talk about his affiliation with them to you. He was worried that you'd tell Conrad and he'd tell his parents."

I set my shovel down. "So why have you let me stay friends with him all these years?"

"He's not a bad kid, Dandra. It's plain to see that he is crazy for you. I like seeing you get the attention you deserve, but his parents are another matter."

"Because they are pro-gaming?"

"Um, yes."

Chapter 25

AS I EAT MY OATMEAL the next morning, I dread
going to school. Conrad will be waiting for me to tell him that
I'm okay with being his girlfriend. Charlisa will be waiting to
hear if I will join the anti-gamers. I can't have both. Am I okay
with having neither? Imagining my life without Conrad and
without my new friends fills me with overwhelming loneliness.
I can't do neither. I can't do both. Which one do I choose?

"Dandra, hurry up. You're going to make me late for
school," Everley says as she drops my backpack onto my empty
oatmeal bowl.

"Sorry, sis. I'm coming," I grumble as I remove the sticky

bowl from my backpack. I wish I had my sister's energy this morning. I can barely keep up with her. Everley pulls hard on my hand to move me faster. When we get to Oak Street, I turn to go the longer way around.

My sister loses all patience with me. "What's wrong with you? We're already late."

I can't look at her face. "I—I don't want to see the blood spot on the road." That's all that she needs to know.

My sister's frustrations melt into sympathy. "Oh—right." She sighs. "It's sad that it happened practically right in front of Conrad's house." Everley pats my shoulder affectionately. "It would make me sad to see where Dad died every time I visited my best friend."

I feel like the earth has started spinning off its axis. How have I been so blind? Dad died—right in front of Conrad's house. Conrad's dad just got his car fixed. Conrad told the patrolmen that Vern did it. Vern says he never took that road but was passed out on his couch. Oh no. Say it isn't so.

I feel like a robot as I walk Everley to the low-level school. She gives me a weird look as I wave and keep walking to the middle-level school. Out of the corner of my eye, I see Conrad walking to the same school entrance that I am. I cannot talk to him right now. I change directions and head to the school's back entrance. Charlisa intercepts me as I walk through the door. "So, are you ready to join us?"

I'm so sick to my stomach, I can't think straight. "I might, but I need to look into my dad's death first."

"This is the perfect time to join us then. We can help you. We don't think his death was an accident."

I'm so confused that all I can do is nod. "I—okay."

"We're meeting at lunch at the same table today. Join us if you want to learn more about your dad's death."

My head nods on its own. "I'll be there."

The bell rings and I wonder if I've done the right thing as I walk to my first class.

Math is a blur. My second class has Conrad in it. I purposely sit between Molly and Jennifer and convince Lori to sit in front of me, so Conrad can't sit by me. I watch him walk in the door. He's still the handsome guy he's always been, and he looks so innocent. He wouldn't help murder my father, would he? The smile on his face turns into a frown when he sees where I'm sitting. He sits two seats in front of me. I look at the back of his spikey black head and feel my veins fill with fire. How could he do this to me? If he helped his parents get rid of my dad, has our whole friendship been a set-up? A fake?

When the bell rings, I bolt out of the classroom, but not fast enough. Conrad grabs my hand in the hall. "What is the matter with you? Why are you mad at me?"

I can feel my face turning red. "Why don't you think about it for a while; if you can't figure it out, I'm sure your parents will know what to do."

Conrad lets go of my hand like I've burned him, and I zip into my English class before he can say anything. I sit in the back corner and lay my head on my desk. My heart is pounding out of my chest. I shouldn't have said anything to Conrad. I don't know if my suspicions are correct. I don't know anything anymore. Someone sets something heavy on my desk. I lift my head up enough to see what it is. It's the book about two-way radios that Baldwin got from the library. He clears his throat. "Hey, I was wondering if you could return this for me at the library today."

"Sure," I say without enthusiasm. I wish Baldwin would tell me everything he knows about my dad. "Hey. Do you have a two-way radio that works?"

"Yep," he says as he opens his book to the poem we'll be discussing.

"Who do you talk to?"

Baldwin glances around the room quickly before answering. "I talked to a man named Stephen from Grainville last week, and a woman named Ernestine, from I'm not sure where, yesterday."

This has nothing to do with my father. I sigh, "Huh. That sounds great."

Baldwin's dark brown eyes search my face. "What's wrong?"

I feel my lips trembling as I say, "I feel like I'm being lied to."

Baldwin rolls his eyes. "You are."

I narrow my eyes at him. "By you?"

He lowers his voice. "No, by people with money and influence."

It's my turn to roll my eyes. "You are a conspiracy theorist. You think we're all being lied to, and I remember you saying that we're all thieves."

Baldwin waits for the teacher to pass back our papers and return to the front of the class before saying, "Yes, I do think that, but that's not what I'm talking about."

"Who's lying to me then?"

"Are you sure you want to know?"

"Yes, I'm sure."

Baldwin leans toward my ear and whispers, "Conrad and his parents."

The spinning sensation I felt on the way to school returns to me. I whisper back, "How do you know?"

He barely moves his lips as he whispers, "Let's just say I eavesdropped on a private conversation at the autobody shop the other day. Do you know why Zane Chesterton needed to have his car fixed?"

"No," I lie as my heart starts pounding in my throat.

"Doesn't it seem weird that they allow their son to hang out with an anti-gamer's daughter?" Did he just call my dad an anti-gamer? He taps his fingers on the radio book. "I'd ask Conrad about that."

My dad didn't like gaming, but he was not a member of this anti-gamer group. I was willing to believe everything Baldwin said until now. "I will. Thank you very much."

Baldwin leans into my ear. "I'm just looking out for you. I don't want you to get hurt."

"Right."

When the bell rings for lunch, I zip out of the classroom faster than everyone else. I grab my wad of tinfoil filled with leftovers and go outside to sit under the apple tree. I have to figure out what I'm going to do before I go sit by somebody in the lunchroom. I feel a tear form in my eye as I take a bite of leftover peas and potatoes.

Someone drops on the ground next to me. "What's wrong?" I hear Conrad's voice ask.

I feel my entire body tense at his presence. "I am trying to have some alone time."

Conrad shakes his head. "I don't know why you took a jab at my parents this morning, and I know you're in a bad mood. I should leave you alone, but I just can't stand watching you suffer by yourself."

He seems so sweet. I just wish it was real. "Conrad, isn't it kind of odd that we became friends? I'm poor and have eccentric parents. You're rich and have an in with any gamer in the city. How did we even meet?"

He lights up. "Don't you remember? I do. We were at a harvest party at the low-level school. You and your dad were playing a trivia game, and no one could beat you. I thought you were so pretty and smart. I was thrilled when my dad insisted that I become friends with you."

My heart drops into my stomach. "It was your dad's idea?"

Conrad shrugs. "Yeah, at first. But I learned quickly that I got the better end of the deal. You were so nice and sweet and pretty." His hand reaches for mine.

I pull my hand away and refuse to let his compliments affect me. "Why do you think your dad wanted us to become friends?"

Conrad shrugs. "He doesn't mingle with the academic crowd too much, so he hoped I'd let him know if anything big was going on," he says, like this is as natural as can be.

I just stare at my best friend's face in shock. "He wanted you to spy on me and my father. I can't believe you just admitted it—our whole relationship is a lie," I spit out as I get up and storm away. Conrad seems stunned for a second, then he tries to follow me.

Charlisa meets me just inside the door. One glare from her stops Conrad in his tracks. I think she just watched that whole interchange. Charlisa takes my arm and leads me inside toward the women's lavatory. "Hey, you said you'd meet with us at lunch to discuss the death of your father."

My mouth twists with frustration. "Yeah, I know. I just don't know what to do with all the questions in my mind right now. Give me more time, please."

Charlisa shrugs. "Okay. I just thought you were ready for answers."

"What answers?"

She clicks her tongue. "We know a kid who was paid to smear some blood on Vern Craigstaff's truck."

"What? Who paid him?"

She shrugs. "He didn't get her name, but she was a well-dressed woman."

Chapter 26

ZELMA INSISTS THAT I TRY her homemade oatmeal-raisin cookies when I get to the library even though I have no appetite. "You are so skinny, when you turn sideways, you practically disappear, young lady. Eat another one."

I take a second cookie and pretend to take a bite with a smile of appreciation. I slip it into my jacket pocket to give to Everley later. "Thanks, Zelma. I plan on finishing the first floor today if I can. Then I can start on that enormous chandelier."

She looks straight up at it and says, "What chandelier? You don't mean this enormous wasp nest, do you?"

I look at the chandelier more closely. It has enough cobwebs on it that it does kind of look like a wasp nest.

Zelma breaks out into a fit of laughter. "Your face was hilarious! You work too hard, darling. It's not worth killing yourself over."

It's that attitude that has made this place such a dump. I force a smile on my face. "I know. I just want to see this place sparkling."

"Me too," a male voice says behind me. It's Baldwin. He brought a short, stocky boy with black hair and glasses with him.

My face slumps into a frown as I look at him. "Can I help you with something?" I say without enthusiasm.

He clears his throat and smiles. "Yes, I need help finding a history book."

Zelma nods at me to take care of him. I roll my eyes. "That won't be possible. That room has been shut down."

Baldwin fakes a look of surprise. "Oh, what a shame. Well, maybe I can get the answer I'm looking for from a book of historical fiction."

I roll my eyes again. He definitely knows that the history section is shut down, and historical fiction isn't going to be a good alternative. "That room is on this floor; right this way, please."

I try to hide my displeasure from Zelma as I skirt around

her desk and lead the two boys into a book room on the far right.

I shut the door behind us and growl, "What do you want?"

Baldwin's eyes look defensive. "Hey, I don't want anything. I'm just trying to help you out."

I turn away from him. "I think I've had all the help I can take for today."

Baldwin raises his hands in surrender. "Don't get mad at me. I was going to do this at lunch, but you never showed up. I just thought you'd like to hear what my friend Hector has to say."

The short, stocky boy has been grimacing at all the dusty books in the room. He is dressed much nicer than Baldwin. When Baldwin elbows him, he puts on a fake smile. "Hello. My name is Hector."

Baldwin rolls his eyes. "How about you tell her where you were the night her father died."

Hector grins and nods. "I was mowing my grandma's lawn on Oak Street when your dad got ran over."

I grab his hand without realizing it. "What? Really? I thought Conrad was the only one who saw the accident."

Hector shakes his head. "Uh, no. I thought I was the only person outside at that time of night. Everyone was inside eating dinner or at the gaming district it seemed like. I was going to go to the gaming district too, as soon as my grandma paid me."

I tug on his arm. "What happened?"

"My lawnmower ran out of gas, so I left it by the edge of the road while I went into the garage to get some more."

My hopes sink. "So you didn't see it happen."

Hector scratches his chin with his free hand. "I didn't see it happen in the moment, but I heard a squealing sound and saw a red car with a dented back bumper stopped in the road. Your dad was on the ground with blood starting to come out of him."

I'm sure my eyes are bulging out of my head as I imagine the scene unfolding. "It was a car, not a pickup?"

Hector pulls his arm out of my grasp. "Yes. I just stood there in shock until a fancy woman in high heels and a dress got out of the passenger seat of the car and walked over to me. She smiled at me and said, 'How would you like to make $1000 today?'

"I said, 'I'd like that very much.' She said, 'I'll pay you $1000 to wipe some of that blood onto the bumper of an old pickup truck a couple blocks away.' I was still in shock, but she seemed so nice and friendly, and I really wanted $1000. So I nodded my head. She took a handkerchief out of her purse and handed it to me. 'Dip this in the blood, and then smear it onto Vern Craigstaff's dented bumper. Do you know who he is?' I nodded my head, which made her smile. She said to burn the handkerchief when I was done and then meet her at the city park to get my money."

Tears are streaming down my face. "So you did exactly what she said?"

Hector shrugged his shoulders. "Yeah. I walked to Vern's house, smeared the blood on his dented bumper, walked home, burned the handkerchief in my backyard, and walked to the park to get my money."

I wipe my eye with the shoulder of my shirt. "Did she pay you?"

"Yeah. She showed up in a taxi and handed me a sack with $1000 in coins, then she said she would give me another $1000 if I promised not to tell anyone anything about what she had me do. So I nodded, and she gave me a second sack with $1000 in it. I went to the gaming district and played until 4:00 in the morning so I wouldn't think about what I had done."

I turn away as a tear rolls down my freshly-wiped cheek. "Why are you telling people now?"

Hector's thick eyebrows crease until they touch. "The lady that paid me the money keeps bothering me with questions when I go gaming. She tells me that I made a promise not to tell anyone about it. Every time I go to the gaming district, she's there watching me. She's ruining the reason I wanted the money in the first place. If she's going to ruin my days, I don't feel bad about ruining hers."

I try to imagine a fancily dressed woman in the gaming district day after day. "Is she a gamer too? Does she always sit by you?" I ask as Baldwin looks at me with pained eyes.

Hector shakes his head and crinkles his nose. "No. She's not a gamer. She works there."

Chapter 27

I STUMBLE HOME FROM WORK the long way. I can't walk by the blood spot next to Conrad's house. I'm almost there when I hear someone behind me. It's dark and it's someone taller than me. I yell out in my tears, "Leave me alone, whoever you are."

Baldwin puts his hand on my shoulder and turns me toward him. "I'm sorry. Are you okay?"

I shake my head. "No. I'm not okay. My best friend lied to me. Not just once—since the day we met. You were right. His dad wanted us to be friends so Conrad could spy on me and my dad."

He lowers his voice. "Zane Chesterton is very good at getting what he wants."

"It appears so."

Baldwins eyes soften while he watches me cry. "Can I help you at all? What can I do?"

I wipe the tears from my eyes and say as seriously as I can, "If this is the beginning of a new friendship, you can do me a favor and not lie to me—ever."

Baldwin's eyes travel down to my clenched fists. "Yeah. That would be the best thing..."

The front porch light of my house turns on as we approach it. My mom calls out the front door, "Dandra, I'm glad you're finally home. Dinner is almost ready, and I could use your help in the shed."

I call back, "Yeah, I'm coming."

Baldwin wipes a tear off my cheek with his finger. "I want to help you figure out what happened that night. Will you let me?"

I glare at him in my misery. "Why? Is it because you owe it to my father's memory?"

He looks hurt. "No. It's because you deserve better. We all deserve better than the corrupt world we live in." His face is full of concern.

I think I'm just an example he wants to use with one of his theories, yet I nod my head. "Okay."

Relief washes over his face. "Will I see you at school on Monday?"

"Yes."

"Will you sit by us at lunch?"

I may as well since I want nothing to do with Conrad for the rest of my life. "Yes."

"Perfect. I'll see you then." His smile is kind as he turns away from me.

I watch him walk quickly away into the darkness before I go inside.

Chapter 28

MOM IS HAVING ANOTHER BAD DAY, and I'm struggling to put my own sad discoveries into words. Was Jerika Chesterton the fancily-dressed woman Hector talked to? It seems like it, but she's not the only fancy woman in this city, right? Conrad's parents aren't the only people around here with a red car...right? My doubts sound feeble, but I have to look into them before I accuse my best friend's family.

I finally put some words together as Mom stirs the pot on the stove. "Mom, I talked to someone named Hector today who says it wasn't Vern's truck that hit dad." Mom turns around and frowns at me. I lick my lips and finish. "He was mowing a lawn on Oak Street that day, and he said it was a red car."

Mom's sad eyes look at me like they can't take much more. "Really? He needs to report that to the patrolman in charge of Dad's case."

"I'll make sure he does."

Her face crumples. "You make sure he does, or I'll report this myself." She breaks down and cries into the soup she's making.

I wrap my arms around her, and we hold each other for a while. Then I make her sit down and eat. Everley watches us with wide eyes the whole time. Mom admits that she hates her job at the bank.

I send Everley to find my heaviest sweater in my room. When she's out of earshot, I say, "Mom, we have to keep working for Everley's sake."

She nods and tells me, "We have to give Grandma some money on Monday. She called today. She's out of food." The tear that rolls down her cheek breaks my heart.

"We'll have some money for her, I promise." Mom smiles at me and sighs as she finishes her soup. Everley enters the kitchen cautiously and hands me my sweater. I smile at her. "Let's go show that tunnel who's boss."

I DECIDE TO TACKLE the chandelier in the library this crisp Saturday morning because we need the money for Grandma. Plus, it will take forever to clean, and I worry that I'll run out of time and strength on a school night. Everley isn't too excited about it. She wants me to stay home with her today.

"I wish I could stay home, but we have a bill that's due on Monday, and I will have enough to pay it if I work today," I explain to her.

"All you care about is bills."

I feel my nostrils flare. "No I don't. You know I'd rather stay home and make cookies with you, but I have a great idea." I put on my jacket and pull out the cookie still in the pocket. We can still have a sister cookie day if you come with me and help me get my work done." Everley reaches for the cookie, but I lift it up so she can't reach it. "Uh, uh. If you want it, you have to commit to be my work buddy today."

She smiles and jumps with her hand outstretched. "Okay, okay. I'll go with you."

I act overly pleased, so she'll feel important. Having a tag along won't make this disgusting job any easier.

Zelma insists that I need a taller ladder than the library owns to clean the chandelier, so she calls the hardware store to see if they will rent us one for the day. Luckily they will, so I just need to get Zelma's desk out of the way before the delivery guy gets here.

Everley is a wonderful help with this job. She takes load

after load of papers and books to the back corner, so the huge, circular desk will be light enough to move. By the time the desk is ready to move, my back is killing me from packing full drawers to the corner. Zelma puts the telephone on the floor next to the circular desk entrance and tells us not to step on it. Everley, Zelma, and I put our backs into the giant wood circle and push with all our might. It moves maybe two inches. This is going to be harder than I thought. We try again and again, but we never move the desk more than two inches.

A couple of stocky boys with GameComs on their arms walk in the door and head to the game cheats room. Zelma stops them in their tracks. "Hey, you. Give us ladies a hand, will ya?" The boys give us a blank stare until Zelma takes their arms and leads them to the desk. "Everybody, push on three. One, two, three!" We shove the desk with all our might, and only get four more inches. Zelma frowns. "Don't tell me that's all the muscle you boys have. Let's try that again. One, two, three." Again, we only move the desk four inches.

Just then the front door opens and the young man who showed me the shovels at the hardware store weeks ago walks in. He pulls a couple of pieces of litter off his legs and shoes and drops them in the trash can by the door. "You ordered a ladder rental?"

Zelma wipes the sweat from her forehead. "Yes, we did. Please bring it in and set it to the side. As you can see, we have to get this desk out of the way before we can set it up." She blinks her eyes several times.

The young man looks around the room and especially at our sweating foreheads. "I can help you with that. If one of you will hold the door, I'll be ready in a minute."

I can see Zelma's face glowing with appreciation. I'm happy to have help too. The young man brings in an enormous ladder with one arm and sets it against the bookshelves to the left. We all get our hands or our backs on the circular desk and after the count of three push again. The young man from the hardware store is on my right, and I can't help but notice how big and strong his muscles are as they flex with each push. In fact, we don't stop this time. The desk just keeps going to the corner until the bookshelves stop us. The boys with the GameComs look at the hardware store worker in awe. My jaw is kind of hanging open too. I close it before anyone else notices.

Zelma places a hand on the young man's arm as she catches her breath. "You are the kind of man that I remember from my youth. All of the men were strong back then. It was a glorious time to live. Thank you for your help, uh, what's your name?"

The young man reaches his muscular arm back to scratch his head. "Uh, I'm Jed."

"How old are you, Jed?"

"I'm 18. I just graduated from middle-level school last year."

"Are you going to go to high-level school at the university?"

"No, ma'am. Now that my dad left us, I'm helping my mom run the store. I don't have time for anything else."

Zelma bites her lip and nods. "Well, that's too bad, but I understand. If you ever get a day off, I'm sure my employee, Dandra, here would love to go to a movie with you."

I kick Zelma in the foot before she can embarrass me more. Jed looks at me, turns red, looks at Zelma, and says, "I will set up this ladder for you, and then I have to be getting back. Saturday is our busiest day at the hardware store."

I don't contradict him even though his mother told me that the hardware store is dead this time of year. He sets up the enormous ladder like it's nothing at all and pulls the litter that is caught on it off and into the garbage can. The GameCom boys watch him do it, shake their heads in amazement, and head to the game cheats room. Zelma writes something on a slip of paper and gives it to Jed with the coins she owes him. He looks at it, then looks at me, blushes, and heads out the door.

I'm at her side in a heartbeat. "What did you write on that piece of paper, Zelma?"

"Your phone number and address," she says with a smile.

I throw my hands up in the air in exasperation. "Are you kidding me? I have all the boy trouble I can handle right now."

"Maybe you've been looking in all the wrong places. He

doesn't look like trouble. He looks perfect." She giggles, and Everley giggles with her.

I smack myself in the forehead. "I can't believe you did that. If you weren't an old woman, I'd never forgive you."

Zelma shrugs. "Well, I am an old woman, so you have to forgive me." She hands me several buckets. "Here are your supplies for the chandelier. Everley can keep refilling the buckets with hot water. And—don't fall off the ladder. You'll uh, have time to think about your choices in men while you're up there."

I shake my head at the much too-involved old woman in front of me. I might have to request the same shifts as Agatha from now on.

Everley brings me a bucket of hot water, and I take it to the top of the ladder. It looks like the chandelier is made of many round sheets of glass with lots of little holes for the crystal shards to stick through. I decide to take all of the cobweb and dust bunny-coated shards out of the bottom sheet of glass and stick them in my bucket of water. I can only reach half of the circle. I take a wet rag and wipe the half of the circle that I can reach top and bottom until it gleams. I then wash all the crystal shards in the bucket and return them to their holes.

As I climb down the ladder with the dirty bucket of water, Everley meets me at the bottom with a fresh, hot bucket of water. She looks up and smiles. "It's already brighter in here, and the chandelier is so pretty."

I look up and nod. "It is pretty. Thanks for the water. If you get bored waiting for me, you can always go in the recipe book room and find a good recipe to make cookies when we're through."

"Okay! I will. Should I look for any certain kind?"

"The kind with few ingredients," I say with a sad smile.

Everley's smile droops. "Okay."

It takes me six hours and several ladder adjustments before I finish cleaning the chandelier. My hands are wrinkly, my back is sore, and my head is throbbing as I climb down the ladder for the last time. I collapse on the floor and look up at my work. Everley drops on the floor next to me and beams. "It looks so beautiful."

I nod. "This whole city used to be that beautiful."

She turns to me. "What happened to it?"

"People don't care about beauty anymore. They just want to play games."

"That's too bad. I like beautiful things."

I turn to her and smile. "Me too. Did you pick out a recipe?"

She nods to a pile of books nearby. "Yeah, I picked four recipes because I'm afraid we don't have the ingredients for some of them."

"As soon as we move Zelma's desk back, we can get out of here."

Zelma waddles over to us and sighs. "What a taxing day.

I'm glad you were the one on the ladder." I smile and shake my head. She nudges me. "I called the hardware store and told them to send Jed to come get the ladder now that we're done with it. I'm sure he'll help us move the desk back."

"There's no need for that. I can do it," Conrad's voice calls out as he steps out from a bookshelf.

I glare at him. "How long have you been here?"

"About 10 minutes."

"Why didn't you help me?"

"You were practically done. It looks great, by the way. I'll have to quit calling this place creepy."

I'm so confused and angry at Conrad for his connection with my dad's death, I want him to feel the pain that I'm feeling. I turn to him. "I'm glad you're here. That desk shouldn't be a problem to move back to the center of the room, right?"

Conrad looks at it and shrugs. "I can move it for you."

I direct him to the far side of the desk and smile. "It helps if you count to three. I'll count for you. One, two, three."

Conrad's GameCom looks like it's in the way as he pushes with all his might. He only gets the heavy desk to move six inches before he stops. "Man, that is heavier than it looks." I try not to laugh.

The front door creaks open, and Jed walks in. He looks at us in the corner and says, "I'll help you put that back as soon as I have the ladder mounted on the truck."

Conrad rolls his eyes at me. "Like he can do any better."

157

I raise my eyebrows. "He lifts heavy stuff all day long. He's very strong."

"It'll take all that both of us can give."

Jed comes back in and walks to the far end of the circular desk. He finds a good spot and starts pushing the desk by himself. Conrad frowns and starts pushing too. It becomes a pushing match between the two of them, but it's pretty clear that Jed is stronger. Once they stop, Conrad looks at Jed while he catches his breath. Jed isn't breathing hard at all.

Zelma gives Jed a look as she says, "You did a beautiful job on that chandelier, Dandra. Now that you're done, you should go do something fun."

Jed turns red, but he looks up and slowly approaches me. "If you have nothing else to do tonight, would you like to go to—"

Conrad interrupts, "Actually, she's on her way to my house now that she's off work. Sorry."

I glare at him and say, "The truth is, I promised my sister that we would make cookies tonight."

"You can make them at my house. My mom has the best-stocked kitchen ever."

Everley pipes in. "I want to make cookies at your house, Conrad."

Jed's red cheeks make him look like he's going to burn alive with embarrassment. "Oh, I didn't know. Maybe another time." He turns around and leaves before I can say a thing.

I'm mad at everyone in the room now. I huff, "Everley, Conrad, and especially you, Zelma, are all terrible! This little girl and I are making cookies at home, and I want you all to stop interfering with my life." Zelma doesn't look sorry at all as she grins at me.

Conrad takes the cookbook in Everley's hand and looks at the page she has her finger in. "Hmm. These cookies take chocolate, caramel, and nuts. Do you guys have all that?"

Everley shakes her head before I can stop her. "No. We don't. That's why I have a plainer recipe in this other book."

Conrad shakes his head. "No way. I know my mom has all of this in our kitchen. You guys should make them at my house."

Everley grins and takes the book back. "These are going to be the best cookies ever!"

I seethe as Conrad smiles at me. I realize how much I love my sister in this moment. It is for her sake, and her sake alone, that I will force myself to enter that house.

Chapter 29

I'M GLAD THAT CONRAD'S PARENTS aren't home when we get to his house. I don't think I could endure this otherwise. His brother, Milo, is sleeping on the couch that he is too big for as we walk through the living room to the kitchen. I look at Conrad's grandfather clock and ask, "Isn't it past four in the afternoon?"

He grins. "Yeah, Milo was unlocking weapons for his best customer, Rupert, until four in the morning."

I try to hide my sarcasm as I say, "That sounds like a healthy lifestyle."

Conrad was right about his kitchen. It is big, beautiful, and well-stocked with anything we could desire. I try not to feel envious as I start pouring things into the mixing bowl. Once the dough is the right consistency, I let Everley make dough balls and put them on the cookie sheet. Conrad takes my arm and wheels me around the corner while she does that. "We need to talk."

I take my arm back. "Yeah, we do."

He looks so confused. "What did I do?"

I don't know if this is the time and place for this discussion, but it has to be discussed some time. "You lied to me about the night my dad died."

Conrad's confused face changes to one of regret. "Why do you think I would lie about that?"

"I think your parents told you to."

His eyes look up and to the left as he says, "My parents had nothing to do with that night."

The old me would just let this go, but I know he is lying, and it's not okay. My teeth grit together. "Yes, they did. Until you can find the courage to tell me the truth, I don't want to talk to you ever again."

Everley comes around the corner just then. "I put the pan in the oven. I hope that's okay."

I force a smile and pat her shoulder. "Of course it's okay. Let's set the timer and get the rest of the dough balls ready so we aren't in Conrad's kitchen when his mom comes back." I shoot him a glare as I take my sister back into the kitchen.

When the first pan of cookies come out, Everley shrieks with delight. "Those are the yummiest looking cookies I've ever seen!"

Conrad acts like nothing is awkward between us when he silently takes a cookie off the pan before they've cooled down and breaks it in half. Gooey chocolate and caramel ooze out before he bites it. It burns his mouth, but I don't feel sorry for him.

"What's that delicious smell?" Milo asks as he waddles into the kitchen yawning.

Everley turns to him and smiles. "Chocolate caramel cookies!"

"Hmm. Those sound good enough to eat." Milo takes a cookie and eats half of it in one bite. "Mmm. These *are* good enough to eat. I better take a whole plate of them and hide them in my room."

Everley shakes her head. "Your mom won't like that. It'll bring in mice."

Milo laughs and tousles Everley's hair. "We don't have mice, and we don't have cookies anymore either, not since the accident—" Conrad steps on Milo's foot and shakes his head. "Anyway, these cookies are the best. I'll just take four or five." He stacks several on his hand and shuffles up the stairs to his room.

I take a cookie and leave Everley to scoop the rest off the pan and put the next set of dough balls in the oven. I walk out the front door and sit on the front porch swing. I can see the blood spot on the road from here. Is that the accident Milo was talking about?

Conrad comes out and sits on the swing next to me. I scoot over as far as I can so I'm not touching him. He looks pained as he looks at me. I look at the blood spot again. I can't stay silent. "So, your mom doesn't bake anymore since the accident. Does she act different in any other ways?"

Conrad looks like his entire body is ripping apart from the inside out. He says slowly, "She—felt so bad about your dad dying on our road. That's why she sent the food for his funeral."

I stop the swing as I plant my feet on the ground. "I don't believe it. I'm tired of being lied to, Conrad. I know your dad set up our friendship so he could spy on my dad, I know he is making a lot of money turning this city into gamer's central, I know my dad opposed that, and I know—that it was his red car that hit my dad."

Conrad turns away from me as his calm face falls apart. "Dandra, where did you hear that?"

"It doesn't matter. Is it true?"

Conrad starts sweating. "N—"

"Conrad—look at me."

"N—yes." I watch his face turn toward me frozen in terror. I sit back in the swing and slowly exhale to calm myself. "You lied to me, Conrad. You are my best friend in the whole world, and you lied to me about the worst event of my life—"

"Dandra—I'm"

I silence him with my hand. "Your dad killed—my dad. I'll never forgive you." I stand up and reach for the door.

Everley comes out at the same time with a plate of cookies. "They're all done now. Do you want another one?"

I take her by the arm and direct her down the steps. "We need to go. Mom is expecting us."

My sister's happy face transforms into an annoyed one. "Okay, okay, don't be so pushy. Goodbye, Conrad. I'll bring back your plate. Thank you."

His eyes barely lift from his feet. "Goodbye," he chokes out as we walk away.

Chapter 30

I FEEL LIKE A ROBOT as I hand my mom my wages and the plate of cookies before I lock myself in my room. I'll tell her, but not until I wrap my head around what Conrad and his father have done. I collapse on my bed and immerse myself in the swirls of paint on my ceiling. He admitted it. I didn't know if he would, but he did. His parents ran over my dad, framed someone else, and lied to everyone about it. I feel so betrayed.

The worst part is—I actually enjoyed our friendship—our fake, pathetic friendship that his dad set up for us. His dad is just like Baldwin said—he's rich, and he gets what he wants, even if it's wrong. I need to tell someone with some power about this.

What if the patrolchief is on Zane Chesterton's payroll? This is going to be messy.

A knock at my door jolts me out of the swamp I'm drowning in. When did it get so dark in here? I open the door to see my mom standing there with a bowl of thin soup. "Are you hungry? You missed dinner."

I let her in and take the soup. It's not much, but it's warm and seasoned well. The soup warms my insides enough to find the words I need to tell her. "Mom, I found something out about Dad's death today."

She looks wary. "You did? From whom?"

I bury my head in my hands as I think about it. "I've had my suspicions ever since I visited Vern Craigstaff in the detainment center."

"What? I didn't know you went to the detainment center."

I take Mom's hand. "Yeah, I was afraid you'd stop me, so I didn't tell you."

Mom surprises me when she says, "Vern must have convinced you that he is innocent."

I nod. "Yeah, he pretty much did. So—I confronted someone today and asked them if they had lied to me, and they admitted that they did."

Mom squeezes my hand and says, "Conrad."

I sit back in shock. "What? How did you know?"

"I've had a bad feeling about Conrad's story from the beginning. Patrolman Mark came by to see me when his brother told him that Zane Chesterton had a dented car in the shop that he works at. He asked me if there was any reason to believe that Zane would want your father dead, and I told him yes. He's been doing some detective work ever since."

Relief washes over me. My mom is trying to find the truth too. "I'm surprised Patrolman Mark has the motivation to help. Why didn't you tell me?"

"Conrad's your best friend, Dandra. You've suffered enough."

I curl up on my bed and wrap my arms around my knees. "You're telling me that Patrolman Mark found out that Conrad lied?"

Mom's shoulders raise. "Well, he doesn't have a confession like you, but he and Vern have been putting the pieces together."

I cover my eyes with my hand. "I feel so used, Mom. Why did I never suspect him?"

"He is your friend, Dandra. He cares about you. I knew his concern for you was real after your father died. That boy never left your side if he could help it."

"He *was* my friend, Mom. He was probably only acting helpful because of guilt."

Mom shrugs. "Maybe. I still think he has more good in him than his parents. Imagine being in his shoes. His dad runs over his girlfriend's dad. Whose side should he take? If he turns his dad in, he no longer has the stable home he's grown up with. If he lies to you about who did it, he can keep his dad out of trouble, and still comfort you."

I feel so tangled up inside. My mom has a great point, but what does that mean for me moving forward? He still lied. Vern is still rotting in the detainment center for no reason, and I want justice for my dad.

"I don't know what to do, Mom."

She wraps her arm around me and places my head on her shoulder. "This is too much for any of us. I think we should leave justice to Patrolman Mark and just be careful what we say and how we act around our friends until justice is served. Can you do that?"

"Yes. At least one thing will be easier."

"What's that?"

"I don't feel bad about giving up Conrad to join the anti-gamers anymore."

Chapter 31

MONDAYS ARE THE WORST. It's so hard to act like life is good on a Monday morning. I take the long way to school again and smile when I meet Charlisa on the way. She gives me a pointed look. "Are you ready to join us yet?"

I look her straight in the eyes. "Yes."

She looks skeptical. "What about Conrad?"

I shake my head. "We aren't friends anymore."

"Huh, that's—great news."

I look down at my feet. "Mmmhmm."

"Meet us at lunch in the school library."

"Why the library?"

"That's where we usually meet, but lately we've been going to the cafeteria to try to recruit you."

"Oh, okay."

"You're sure that Conrad won't come looking for you, right?"

"I'll make sure he doesn't."

I'M NERVOUS AS I ENTER my history class. Conrad will be in here. What do I do? Barricade myself again? It's tempting, but then he might try to find me later. I better just talk to him now, so he knows for sure that I don't want anything to do with him anymore.

I sit right in the middle of the classroom next to no one and wait to see what happens. When Conrad comes in, he looks like he's been hit by a bus. His usually perfect spikey hair is messy. He has dark rings under his eyes, and his clothes look wrinkled, like he slept in them. As a matter of fact, he wore that outfit yesterday. He did sleep in them. When he looks at me, I look down at my desk. He sits in the desk to my left and looks straight ahead.

Mr. Henry is super concerned about the educational amendment the country is about to vote on in a couple of weeks. He tries to convince the class that their parents should vote to keep the graduation age the same. No one in the class seems to be buying it, though.

A boy named Matt raises his hand and says, "I can't wait to be done with school. If we can be done this year, our lives will be so much easier!" The class erupts in applause.

Mr. Henry quiets everyone down and explains all the learning we'll miss out on if we quit now. The gamers in the class don't agree, and a full-on debate breaks out. I glance to the left to see what Conrad is doing.

He's looking straight at me like his puppy just died. He mouths, "I'm sorry, Dandra." The class is in such an uproar that no one sees or hears us.

I lean toward him and whisper, "Sorry doesn't cut it." His eyes drop to his desk. I have so much to say, I hope I don't forget anything. "You heard me say that I was going to march up to Vern Craigstaff and tell him that he ruined my life. You said you watched him drive drunk right into Dad. I'm such an idiot. You and your rich, powerful family are the ones who ruined my life. The saddest part is you've got enough money to keep the truth from being known. I know that it's too late for my dad, but Vern has had his life taken away too. That is not okay. Ever. I can never trust you again. We can never be friends."

He leans toward me. "Dandra, I was so careful how I said it. I said 'he' was drunk, but I didn't say that the 'he' I was talking about was my dad. I wasn't lying when I said drunk drivers don't know what they're doing half the time. It was an accident. Wouldn't you try to help your parents if they did something on accident?"

I turn my head to him long enough to say, "If the situation was reversed, my parents wouldn't ask me to lie for them."

Conrad looks like he is about to break. "They were wrong, Dandra. I see that now. There were so many decisions being made in a matter of minutes. It wasn't handled right. I'm so sorry. I hope one day you'll forgive me."

I shake my head. "I don't know if that can happen. Once justice is served, I'll at least consider it."

He looks alarmed. "Are you going after my parents? That may not be a good—"

I fire back, "Someone is. I hope you get the chance to live without your father, just like me."

Conrad's face crumples, and as soon as the bell rings, he's gone.

I sit there for a minute calming my pounding heart. I thought I would feel victorious, but instead I feel—empty.

Chapter 32

BALDWIN SITS BY ME in English again. I guess we are best friends now. He smiles at me. "I heard you dumped your boyfriend. That's a good thing. We have so much to catch you up on now that he's out of the way."

I twirl my pencil around my finger. "Like what?"

He leans toward me conspiratorially. "Like how his parents have paid off half the patrolmen in town, the judge, the body shop, Hector, and possibly a few more."

I collapse onto my arms. "How can we compete with that kind of money?"

Baldwin opens his book and stares at it. "We can't bribe

anyone, but we have ways to find out information without money."

I mumble through my arms, "What, like two-way radios?"

He looks at me and nods. "Um, yeah, among other things."

The teacher approaches us and puts her hands on her hips. "If you two can't quit talking in class, I'll have to separate you."

Baldwin pipes in without missing a beat. "I was just debating with Dandra whether this story is an epic poem or not. I'm 99% sure that it is."

Our teacher gives him an indulgent smile. "You're right, it is. I was hoping someone in this class would notice." She taps his desk and walks away.

I look at Baldwin in amazement. "I don't know how you just did that, but wow. You have skills."

He smiles and winks at me. "Yes, and I read."

AT LUNCH Charlisa, Adamar, Baldwin, a tall, dark guy named Gordon, a short, stocky guy named Ed, and a tiny, shy girl named Marcella sit with me in the school library. I feel so included and involved. It's weird, but nice.

Baldwin seems to be the leader. He introduces us all and then asks me if I have any questions. I remember Conrad's opinion about them and ask, "Have you guys shut down the power to the gaming district before?"

Ed's long blonde hair bounces as he nods. "Yeah, twice."

Gordon scratches between his black corn rows and says, "We meant to shut down the power for good, but we didn't know how many generators they have on standby. It's insane."

I want to ask if they are all homeless, but it feels like a rude thing to ask, so I don't. Their clothes are pretty worn, though.

Baldwin clears his throat. "Okay, let's not tell that long and boring story at this first meeting. Let's focus on the task at hand. We need to prove that Zane Chesterton killed Gifford Metty and framed Vern Craigstaff for it."

Gordon rubs his hands together. "I wish we had a hidden radio inside that huge house of theirs. I'm sure they talk about covering their tracks all the time."

I nod in agreement. "Yeah, they probably do. But I could probably get Conrad to talk about it again."

Baldwin looks at me in astonishment. "Wait, he told you that he lied to the patrolmen?"

I tighten my ponytail. "Yeah, he did. By the way, there is a patrolman named Mark who is investigating my dad's death. Hector needs to talk to him."

Baldwin leans back in his chair. "Ed can arrange that, right?"

Ed nods excitedly. "Oh yeah, I'll get right on that."

Baldwin twirls a pencil in his fingers, like I sometimes do, as he thinks. "I bet we could figure out a way to record him talking to you. I can't believe he told you the truth. He's been telling his dad all of Gifford's secrets for years."

"How do you know?"

"We have our sources. Plus, Gifford used to have some pretty deep conversations with us, right, gang?"

They all nod and say, "Yeah."

I shake my head. "No one but my dad himself knew all of his secrets."

Baldwin shrugs. "Well, sure, but Conrad told Zane enough to make him want to get rid of your dad."

Secrets. What a dangerous word. I lower my eyes to the dirt under my fingernails. "Apparently. I just don't think Conrad told his dad everything he knew."

Chapter 33

MOM IS SUCH A STRONG, determined woman. She is hacking away at the dirt in the tunnel almost as fast as Dad did, with half the time available. As I'm helping her, I reflect back to my earlier thought at lunch time. Why hasn't Zane Chesterton sent any of his paid patrolmen to destroy this tunnel?

"Mom, Conrad knows about this tunnel. He's known about it for years."

"Yeah, I know."

"The anti-gamers told me that Conrad's dad has paid off the judge and some of the patrolmen."

Mom wipes the sweat off her forehead with her arm. "That's probably true."

I look at the dirt walls around me. "Why hasn't his dad sent his paid patrolmen to destroy this yet?"

Mom sets her shovel down and leans on the handle. "Well, I can think of two reasons. One, he may not care that your dad wanted to leave. He might have wanted your dad to leave the country so he could carry on with his gaming plans unopposed."

"Huh, I guess that makes sense. What else could it be?"

Mom looks at me like I'm slow in the head. "Maybe Conrad didn't tell him."

I scoff, "No, that can't be it. Spying on dad is the only reason Conrad became my friend, Mom. Our friendship was a fake. He doesn't care about me."

Mom doesn't look convinced. "That's what you keep saying, baby girl."

It's time to talk about something else. "How do you think the vote will go next week for the educational amendment?"

Mom starts hacking dirt up high on the wall. "I don't know. The people at work are about 50/50 on it."

Some loose dirt falls on my head. I shake like a dog to get it out. "I feel like Dad would want us out there convincing people to vote to keep us in school, but with school and work, I don't have time for that."

Mom nods. "I know, darling. We may not have the time or platform to help the cause, but we can at least stick to our beliefs and talk to our friends and co-workers about the cons of less education."

"Yeah. I'll talk to Agatha and Zelma about it."

I'm in complete shock when my mom breaks out into giggles. When she finally composes herself, she says, "You tell them, Dandra."

I laugh as I think about the two old ladies I work with. Those two and—Conrad have been my world. I wish that talking to Conrad's parents about the vote would do any good, but that ship has sailed. It's a sobering thought.

I shudder. "I'm liking this country less and less all the time. Let's get this tunnel finished and get out of here."

Chapter 34

SOMETIMES I LONG for my days of innocence and ignorance. I used to walk to school with Conrad, laughing and joking, without a worry in the world. Now I take the long way to avoid him. I barricade myself in class so I won't have to sit by him. I cringe at all the new dirt I find out about Conrad's family at lunchtime. Life is exhausting now.

In English class, when I tell Baldwin how I'm feeling, he nods and thinks before responding. "So, you'd rather be happy in ignorance, than sad in the truth?"

"Well, y—I don't know. I guess—not."

"I can't speak for you, but I would rather have the truth, no matter how horrible it is, every time."

I sigh. "Yeah, you're right. It's just hard when the truth is constantly heartbreaking."

"You've had more than your fair share of heartbreak. We—should do something happy—together sometime."

I look at him curiously. "Like what?"

He taps his pencil on his chin while he thinks. "Like go swimming at the city pond."

Hasn't he noticed that the leaves are falling off the trees? "No way. It's too cold and too dirty."

He concedes easily. "Okay, how about flying kites on the hill by the cemetery?"

No one has ever suggested an activity like that to me before. I wrap my hair around my finger and grin as I imagine it. "Maybe."

His eyes light up. "Or, if you can be out late, I have a telescope. We could go stargazing."

The thought floods me with emotion. I used to do that with my dad when I was a little kid. I loved it. I look at Baldwin, who has no idea how I'm feeling. "I'm pretty sure my dad has—had—a telescope too. It's probably in his office. I'd like to do that."

"Okay, how about Wednesday?"

Huh, he's serious about this. "Yeah. That would be great. Do you want to meet at your house or mine?"

He looks down at his green sneakers. "Uh, I'd rather meet at your house, or go straight to the city park."

I wish he'd just tell me that he's homeless. "Um, just pick me up at my house—then neither of us will sit around hoping we're at the right place by ourselves."

He smiles. "Okay, I'll pick you up at 9:30 pm; it's a date."

His words strike me. It's a date? Is that what this is? I look at Baldwin again, differently this time. He has a pleasant face. His eyes are dark brown, and they crinkle when he smiles. His thick brown hair could use a haircut still, but it's not horrible. I feel something, but it's not discomfort. I think it's excitement.

Chapter 35

AGATHA IS AS HAPPY as I've ever seen her when I walk into the library after school. She says, "The chandelier looks very nice. I had forgotten how lovely it used to be. It's the finishing touch for the first floor. I've had so many happy patrons compliment me about it today. Good work."

I scuff my shoes together as her praise washes over me. "Thank you." I look up at the railing around the third floor. "Should I start on the third floor again, or should I work on the attic or the basement?"

Agatha takes off her bejeweled spectacles and cleans them on her skirt. "Let's have you start on the attic, and then move to the basement. Once those are done, you can start over on the third floor, until—you know." She gives me a knowing look.

I nod. "Until the mayor cuts more funding."

"Yes."

I look up to the atrium ceiling. "Okay. What should I expect to find up there?"

Agatha slides her glasses up her nose. "I'm not exactly sure. I haven't been up there in 10 years. I can't remember. If you find anything good, bring it down to me. The hidden staircase is in the ceiling of the religious books room."

I pull my hair back into a ponytail as I imagine how thick the dust must be up there. "Okay, I'll bring down a surprise for you."

When I pull down the hidden staircase to the attic, dust particles rain down on me and my newly-cleaned book room. Oh boy. It takes me 40 minutes just to clean up the tiny staircase and the dust mess on the floor. This is going to be gross.

The attic is one solid blanket of gray dust. My feet leave brown holes in the dust blanket as I walk around the huge room. The ceiling is triangular and so low that I accidentally hit my head on it as I examine an old music machine against the wall. My eyes catch another brown spot in the room. A closet on one side somehow had someone open the door recently because the dust is pushed away. I don't see footsteps anywhere besides mine though. Huh. The floor of the closet has dust pushed away too, and though it's dark in here, I can see a hole in the floor, big enough for an animal or a small person to fit through.

I call down the hole, "Hello?" I don't hear anything. Agatha is probably the only person in the building anyway. I wonder if there are rats or raccoons crawling through the walls of this enormous old building. Ugh. There aren't any droppings up here, but I'm suddenly dreading the thought of cleaning the basement. I hope Agatha's rat traps have been successful.

I sigh as I realize how much hot water I'll have to haul up the little staircase to get this room clean. Three buckets at a time should save me some steps.

My plan works out okay. I only spill on myself—every single time. Besides the old music playing machine, I find boxes of books written in another language, old-fashioned chairs, and—an old-fashioned vacuum cleaner! The thick blanket of dust will disappear so much faster if this thing works....I plug it in as my hands shake with excitement. Unfortunately, it doesn't work. I examine the long tube and find a wad of feathers stuck in it. As I pull the wad out, I realize there are bones in the feathers. Ew! I drop the dead bird on the floor and decide to just stick with hot water and rags.

"Dandra, are you up there?" I hear a male voice call up the trapdoor hole.

I walk over to the hole and look down into Baldwin's face. "Oh, hey, Baldwin. I'm here."

He looks at me sheepishly. "Can I come up?"

I look at the majority of the room still covered in dust and the dead bird by the broken vacuum cleaner and shrug. "Sure, I hope you're not afraid of dust."

Baldwin's tall, thin body rises through the trapdoor hole and takes in the room like it's the most natural sight in the world. "It looks like you have your work cut out for you up here. The rest of the library looks great, by the way." He starts snooping around into the things I've uncovered.

I wash my hands in a bucket of water and wipe them on my shirt. "I was trying to get the old vacuum cleaner I found working, but I found a dead bird in it and gave up."

Baldwin sets down the foreign language book that he is looking through and walks over to the vacuum cleaner. "I bet I can figure it out. I've used one just like this before."

I laugh. "I can't believe another one of these exists anymore."

Baldwin smiles at me. "Believe it." He pulls a few more random things out of the tube, empties the bag that collects dirt, fiddles with a black belt, and—turns it on.

I wipe my hands on my grungy t-shirt and laugh. "How did you do that?"

He shrugs. "Like I said, I read a lot."

"What were you reading over there? Those books are written in another language."

His grin is as big as a crescent moon. "Yeah, I'm so excited that you found those. "They are written in Greek and Latin. I've searched this library top to bottom looking for them. I thought they were thrown out."

I know where they could have been. "Or just locked up in one of the boarded-up rooms."

Baldwin shakes his head. "Naw, I knew they weren't in there."

I shake my head in disbelief. "You memorized every book in those six rooms before they were boarded up?"

Baldwin's eyes dart around the room. "Uh, like I said, I read a lot."

"Why are you here? I doubt you knew I would need help with a vacuum."

"Yeah—I just wanted to make sure your mom was okay with our 9:30 pm date tomorrow."

Date. He and I are going on a date tomorrow. I twist my hands in my t-shirt. "She was fine with it." Oops. I haven't had the chance to tell her about it. I'm sure it'll be fine. I flatten my shirt and look at him. "Should I bring anything besides my dad's telescope?"

He puts his hands in his pockets. "Yeah, dress warm, and could you bring a blanket to sit on?"

"Sure."

He smiles. "Perfect. So, once you're done cleaning the attic, are you done working here, or will you start dusting everything all over again?"

I look around the room at the blanket of dust remaining.

"I'll start dusting everything all over again once I've finished the basement."

Baldwin doesn't look at me as he fidgets with the vacuum cleaner cord. "I'm surprised to hear that. I thought the library was out of money."

"It is. Agatha found a little bit of money in a long-lost janitorial budget, but most of my money comes out of her paycheck."

"That is nice of her."

I dip my rag into the water bucket. "Yeah, we're both hoping that the mayor will be impressed with how the library looks when he comes for their next meeting and stop cutting the budget."

Baldwin wanders back to the box of Greek and Latin books. "Yeah, we all better hope that he stops cutting the heating budget—and other things."

I rub my goose-bump-free arms. "Is it that cold in here? I guess I move so much while I'm working, I don't think it's cold."

Baldwin picks up the book he was looking at earlier. "It's not that bad now, but it can get pretty chilly at night."

"Huh, I'll have to pay closer attention."

Baldwin fidgets with the vacuum handle for a minute. "Dandra, when do you think you'll start on the basement?"

I shrug. "Probably Thursday or Friday. Do you want to take any of those Greek books with you? I bet Agatha would check them out to you."

Baldwin looks at the closet door with the dust-free opening and shrugs. "I'll take one. I have plenty of time to check out the rest of them." He picks up the next book in the box and switches it with the one he's holding. He turns toward the trapdoor. "I better let you get back to work. I don't want Agatha to give up her paycheck for nothing." He winks at me and climbs down the stairs with the book in his hand. "See you tomorrow, Dandra."

My stomach flip flops. "Okay. Bye."

The smile on my face doesn't budge as I vacuum the remaining blanket of dust off the attic floor.

Chapter 36

EVERLEY HELPS ME FIND my dad's telescope in his old office when I get home. She's never used it, so I promise to show her after Baldwin shows me on our—date. Being in my dad's office doesn't make me as sad as I thought it would. I find a box of drawings that I'd given him and he had saved since I was old enough to hold a pencil. I can't believe he kept them. I find his notes on the political movements in the country and the speeches he gave about the dangers of gaming, some of which were labeled as speeches for the "anti-gamers," but best of all, I find his journal. The first page brings me to tears as I read about how excited he was for Everley's birth after they had given up hope of having another child. Reading the words, "My daughters are my most prized treasures. They make this world a better place by just being in it," reminds me of his loving voice and twinkling eyes. I could never find a better dad, not if I searched for a thousand years. I just wish he was still here.

My sister's voice is so soft, I almost miss what she says. "Dandra, if you're going on a date with Baldwin, does that mean that you don't like Conrad anymore?" she asks.

I force myself back to the present. As I look at my sister's frowning face, I realize that this might be the easiest way to explain why I'm not hanging out with him anymore. "Yeah. Well, I never liked Conrad as more than a friend, but I think he liked me more. We have—parted ways now. So, please don't go to his house or talk to him about me if you see him, okay?"

Everley doesn't look impressed. "That's stupid. He's always nice to us, and you know it." She turns around and slams the door on the way out.

Mom isn't thrilled that my late-night date is on a school night, but she seems okay with it otherwise. She likes the educational aspect of it at least. She finds me a book about the features of the moon from Dad's bookshelf. "Really focus on the maria of the moon through the telescope. My favorite one is Mare Crisium sitting away from the rest. You'll have to tell me which one is your favorite."

"Okay, Mom. I will."

While Everley sulks at the table as she does her

homework, Mom helps me curl my hair and pick out the cutest warm clothes that I have. She picks out two blankets to send with me because she doesn't want us to share one. If I wasn't sweating enough, my armpits start pouring when she mentions that.

All three of us jump when we hear a knock at the door at exactly 9:30. As Mom goes to answer it, she says, "At least he's punctual." I roll my eyes.

When the door opens, I am pleasantly surprised with what I see. Baldwin has a nice-looking haircut, a bigger telescope than mine, and he brought Charlisa and Adamar with him. He smiles at me as they walk in. "I hope you don't mind some extra company."

I smile at everyone. "Of course not. This will be fun!"

Baldwin sticks out his hand to my mom. "It's nice to meet you, Mrs. Metty. I'm Baldwin Kole. I was a big fan of your husband's work."

Mom nods at him and looks at the other two. I pipe in, "This is my friend Charlisa and her friend Adamar."

Adamar looks at Charlisa then at me and smiles. "Maybe someday I'll be your friend too, huh, Dandra?"

I smack him in the arm. "Of course, you're my friend. You and Charlisa just...know each other better."

Mom clears her throat. "I hate to be a party pooper, but even though you need a late-night sky to do this—it is a school night, so I want Dandra back home before midnight."

"That won't be a problem, Mrs. Metty," Baldwin assures her as he takes the telescope from me. "Thank you for letting us use this."

Mom hands him the book about the moon. "You'll want this book too." I cringe, but Baldwin takes the book and thanks her graciously. Adamar takes one of the blankets. I take the other and breathe a sigh of relief as we leave my house behind.

Baldwin leans toward me as we walk behind Charlisa and Adamar. "Why didn't your sister leave the table while we were there?"

"She was doing her homework."

He doesn't let it drop. "She wouldn't stop frowning. Does she hate homework?"

I shake my head. "No, she just—had a bad day. She needs to sleep it off." He doesn't question me more about it.

The world is so quiet at night. I kind of like it.

"This looks like a good spot, don't you think?" Baldwin asks as he sets both telescopes down in the middle of the park's open field. "I don't want trees to block our view."

"Yeah, this is great," I say as I open the blanket I'm holding over the trash on the lawn.

Adamar takes the bigger telescope, sets it up, and has the knobs adjusted in a matter of minutes. He must use Baldwin's stuff a lot. Baldwin takes his time making sure he gets my dad's telescope set up correctly. He nods at it once it's lined up.

"There we go. With the moon almost full, we have a perfect view of Mare Crisium. Check it out."

I am hyper-aware of Baldwin's proximity as I look into the telescope. "That's my mom's favorite maria." It is a beautiful sight. It makes me feel like I'm part of something bigger than my little city and its problems. When I pull my eyes away, Baldwin is looking at me.

"What?"

He smiles. "I just like how much you know about the moon's features."

I'm glad it's dark so he can't see my cheeks turn red. "I used to do this with my dad when I was a kid. Can your bigger telescope see more than mine?"

He shrugs. "A little bit. It's an older telescope though."

Adamar switches us, and I look through Baldwin's telescope. The moon is a little bit clearer in this one than in mine. "Where did you get this?"

"Uh, in the—trash."

I fold my arms in front of me and frown. "What a wasteful thing for someone to do. I'm glad you found it."

Baldwin pats the telescope like it's a dog. "Yeah, it's becoming a hobby of mine."

I try not to laugh. "Digging through the trash?"

Baldwin laughs. "No, taking educational equipment that no one else wants anymore."

I remember what my dad said about people stealing books

from the university. "Have you ever taken anything from the high-level school?"

He nods. "Yeah, they throw out books and lab equipment all the time."

I still don't know if he is part of the group my dad told me about before he died. "You always have permission to take things, don't you?"

Baldwin tilts his head to the side. "Yes, Dandra. I'm not a thief."

I'm not sure that's true. "Wait a second, you told me at school not too long ago that we are all thieves in one way or another."

Baldwin stops in his tracks. "You're right. I did say that. I believe it too. There is so much knowledge and—resources for the taking if we are willing to reach out and grab it."

"I'm just glad you don't steal books."

Baldwin looks sideways at Adamar. "Um, yeah. Do you know your constellations? Let's lay on the blanket and see how many we can find."

My heart starts beating faster as I lay on the blanket next to Baldwin. I like the smell of his woodsy-scented cologne. I sneak a peek at him and catch him looking at me. He quickly turns his face up toward the stars. "I see Queen Cassiopeia."

"Where?"

He points into the air. "Do you see the bright 'W' shape to the lower left?"

"Oh, yeah."

He looks at me again. "What do you see?"

I force my eyes upward. "I see the North Star shining brightly. I can see the Big Dipper!"

Adamar scoffs. "Even a child can find the Big Dipper."

Baldwin throws a wad of trash at his friend. "Shut up, Adamar." His eyes shine in the moonlight as he asks, "Can you see the Little Dipper?"

I scan the sky until I see it. I point to it. "Yep. There it is."

He turns toward me and smiles. His haircut really makes him look nice tonight. I'm pretty sure I can hear the other two kissing beside us, but I don't want to turn my head to find out. Baldwin calls to Adamar and Charlisa on the next blanket over. "What do you guys see besides each other?"

Adamar throws the moon book at Baldwin. "Give us a break. We never get to spend time together away from prying eyes."

"I know, but I won't invite you again if that's all you're going to do. And you need to be careful with Dandra's book."

Adamar sits up, looks closely at the stars, and points. "There's Scorpius."

Charlisa lays her head on his shoulder and points upward. "There's Cygnus. Is anyone ready for hot chocolate?"

Baldwin sits up and asks excitedly, "Did you bring some?"

"Yeah. I knew you guys wouldn't bring anything, and it would be cold, so I filled up a thermos before I left."

I'm not surprised when Adamar and Charlisa share the cup that doubles as a lid to the thermos, but when Baldwin drinks out of it too and hands it to me, I'm not sure what to think.

"None of us are sick. Drink up," he insists. So I do.

Is this how homeless people are? They don't care about germs. They just share everything? I'm curious. "I thought your mom didn't like you hanging out with Adamar, Charlisa."

She snorts. "She doesn't, but she agreed to let me come tonight because this is an extra-credit school assignment," she says as she makes quotation marks with her fingers.

I snicker, "Sneaky girl. Where do you live?"

"On Pine Street, not too far from you-know-who on Oak Street."

The smile on my face melts off. I don't want to think about Conrad right now. I turn to Baldwin. "So where do you live?"

Baldwin and Adamar's eyes meet as he thinks for a minute. "I live on Main Street."

I'm kind of surprised to hear that. "Really? That explains why I see you in the library so much; it's on Main Street too."

Baldwin wraps the end of the blanket around our legs. "Yep, I think of the library as my neighbor." Adamar sniggers into Charlisa's hair.

I inch toward him slightly. "You'll have to show me where you live someday after work."

Baldwin squirms. "Yeah, someday."

Charlisa pours more hot chocolate. "Who wants more?" We all do, so we pass it around again.

I lay back down on the blanket and let the stars envelop me in their twinkly wonder. I whisper, "The stars are so beautiful. I should take the time to enjoy them more."

Baldwin lays down beside me. "We all should, but life gets busy and complicated sometimes."

I exhale. "You can say that again."

He picks a piece of garbage out of my shoelaces. "Has Patrolman Mark found out anything new?"

"Not that I know of."

"I've been working hard every night the past week, and I think I have a device you could hide on yourself so you can record Conrad confessing that he lied about Vern. Are you willing to try it?"

I think about it for a minute. "Yeah. I think I am."

Baldwin takes my hand and gives it a squeeze. "It's 11:30. We better pack up and get you home."

I feel disappointed. I could stay out here so much longer. "Okay." He lets go of my hand and sits up to put away the telescope. I fold the blanket. After a gentle kick from Baldwin, Adamar quits kissing Charlisa and puts away the other telescope. Charlisa sighs as she folds the other blanket.

When we get to my front gate, Baldwin leans in and kisses my cheek gently. "Good night. I hope we can do something like this again sometime."

I'm so flustered, I forget how to speak. "Yeah. Good night."

Chapter 37

I CAN'T STOP YAWNING as I get ready for school. I couldn't sleep last night. I could still feel the spot where Baldwin kissed my cheek, and my mind kept replaying the whole night to the tiniest detail. I keep thinking about how different that kiss was to the kiss from Conrad. I didn't stay up all night thinking about that kiss. It wasn't unpleasant, but it didn't leave me tingly either. What is the difference?

I think Baldwin likes me—maybe not as much as Conrad did, but he cut his hair for our date. He held my hand for a minute, and he kissed my cheek. He has to like me, right? So if they both like me, why is it different this time? I think—I like Baldwin back.

I find some spring in my step as I come down the stairs for breakfast. There are three omelets in a pan on the table. One of them is broken up and overcooked on the edges. Everley dishes that one onto my plate and smiles cruelly, which turns my smile into a frown. Mom digs into her omelet in a hurry. "We are running a little bit late, girls. Eat up. How was your date last night?"

A smile erupts onto my face without any effort. "It was great. The sky was clear, the hot chocolate was delicious, and the company was fun."

"So which maria was your favorite?"

"Um—I'm with you, Mom. Mare Crisium is my favorite too." Mom nods appreciatively.

Everley stabs her next bite a little bit harder than is needful. "Making cookies at Conrad's house was more fun than that."

No. No, it wasn't, little sister. "Everley, you don't know all the bad things that Conrad and his parents have done. I have good reasons for staying away from him."

She glares at me. "Everybody makes mistakes."

"He told a terrible lie to me, Everley."

She looks out the window. "Janae lied to me once too, but we're still friends."

Mom clears her throat. "We don't have time to talk about

this now. You have one minute to finish your breakfast, and then you have to run to school."

Everley and I both mumble, "Okay, Mom," and finish our omelets.

When we open the front door to leave, we're surprised to see a bouquet of purple asters in a simple glass cup on the porch. Mom smiles and grabs the white card sitting next to them. Her smile fades as she says, "They're for you, Dandra." I don't even have to look at the card to know who they're from. These flowers grow wild in every empty lot in Tifton, especially in the fall. Conrad would never give me something so common and cheap. I pick them up and smile at the thought and effort it took to have these ready this early in the morning. These are from Baldwin.

I AM ON CLOUD NINE ALL MORNING LONG. I don't even think about Conrad's sad face as I take my history quiz. I count down the minutes until I can see Baldwin in English. His smile when I walk through the door is worth a million coins to me, and he's saved me a seat.

The dark circles under his eyes don't detract from their brilliance. "How are you this morning? Not too tired, I hope."

I smile and shake my head. "I didn't sleep much, but I'm

not tired." I feel my face get warm as I think about my surprise this morning. "Thank you for the flowers."

He grins at me. "No problem. I'm glad you liked them."

I don't know why, but it seems like everyone in the classroom's eyes are on us today. I don't care though. We get our vocabulary assignments done in half the time of everyone else, so we have time to talk.

Baldwin whispers into my ear, "When should I bring you the recording device? I assume you still want to free Vern."

I whisper back, "Oh yeah. You could bring it to the library after school. I'll be finishing the attic today."

"Perfect. I'll bring it then."

When the bell rings, I love that I don't have to say goodbye to him. He follows me to my locker to get my lunch, and then we walk to the school library together. I can't wipe the smile off my face. Is this what having a boyfriend is like? If it is, I could definitely get used to it.

THE ATTIC OF THE LIBRARY is so much better since I vacuumed it yesterday. I just have to dust and wash off the other items in the room now. I fill with delight when a big round ball of cobwebs and dust turns into a globe of the earth as my rag washes it off. It is amazing how big the world is. I've rarely left my city, let alone my country, but there are so many countries I'd like to visit. Looking at the United Cities right next to Layland makes me want to finish the tunnel even more. I'm glad this globe wasn't in the map room when they boarded it up.

"Dandra, are you up here?" Balwin's voice calls up the staircase.

"Yes, come on up," I call out as I finish wiping down a wooden chair.

He is so tall and handsome as he ascends the staircase. How did I never notice him until now? Even his voice is breathtaking. "Here is the recording device I made for you. You just clip the microphone part to the collar of your shirt. Hide the rest of it in your pocket or in your—under uh, clothes." His blush is kind of adorable. "Twist this knob to 'on' when you're ready to record. I'd do it before you approach him."

I lick my lips nervously. "Okay. How do I make an excuse to talk to him?"

"I'm sure he'd meet you anywhere for any reason. It won't be hard for you."

I wrinkle my nose. "I'm not so sure."

Baldwin raises his eyebrows. "He's still crazy about you."

I was pretty mean to him the last time we talked. I duck my head as I remember that conversation. "How can you tell?"

He rubs his shoulder self-consciously. "Well, he pushed me into the wall after school today and told me to stay away from you. I think that's proof enough."

I'm stunned. "Really? I'm so sorry. I guess I'll try to record him soon. Are you okay?"

Baldwin brushes it off. "Yeah. No big deal. I don't let gamers push me around."

Curiosity overwhelms me. "What—did you say to him?"

He shrugs. "I said that he didn't own you, and that I'd hang out with you if I wanted to."

I try to hide the smile that wants to erupt onto my face. "I'm sure he loved that."

He smiles at me. "Yeah, well, Mr. Henry walked up to us just then, so he just walked away."

I smile in spite of my horror. "I'm so sorry."

"Like I said, it's not a big deal. You're worth it." He gently touches the curve of my cheek when we hear Agatha calling up the stairs.

"Dandra, is there an extra chair up there? I, uh, accidentally broke one down here."

I feel flustered as I look around the attic. "Yes. I'll bring one down," I call back. Baldwin picks up the chair I just dusted and offers to carry it down for me.

"I better be going. Are you starting the basement tomorrow?"

I look around at what still needs to be done. "Yes, if I get the rest of this done tonight."

Baldwin nods. "It's a big job. I'll have to tell you about my job sometime."

"You have a job?"

"Yep." He leans over and pecks my cheek before squeezing down the pull-down staircase with the chair. "I'll see you tomorrow."

"Yeah. See ya." That little spot on my cheek raises at least 50 degrees; I feel like it might start on fire.

Chapter 38

MOM STARES AT ME as I eat my oatmeal. "What?" I ask through my mouthful.

She cocks her head as she looks at me. "You seem different. You're unusually happy the last few days."

Her comment just makes me want to smile more. "I am happy. It's nice to have something to smile about again."

She gives me a knowing look. "Is Baldwin the reason you're smiling?"

"Um—yeah."

Everley slams her spoon on the table and glares at me.

Mom shakes her head at Everley and then looks at me.

"Please be careful. You've been through a lot lately, and I don't want you to jump into a relationship just because you have a hole in your heart that needs filling."

Is she serious? "Mom, I'm not stupid."

"I know. I just want you to know that I care about you."

Knock, knock. Everley jumps out of her seat and runs to the door. She's scowling when she walks back with a dozen roses in a vase. I smile in anticipation, but Everley sets the vase down in front of my mom. She opens the card and smiles.

I can hardly contain my curiosity. "Who are they from?"

"Patrolman Mark."

Yikes. Where have I been? My words are slow and full of venom when I say, "I wondered why a lazy patrolman would offer to help us out. How can you trust him?"

Mom is immediately defensive. "He is the least lazy patrolman I have ever met. He is very nice and is helping us out a lot. I don't want to hear another negative thing out of your mouth about him."

I jump to my feet. "I can't believe this. Dad is not even cold in his grave yet, Mom!" I grab my backpack, my jacket, and my sister and slam the door on my way out.

I look at Everley and huff, "Can you believe Mom?"

She glares at me and says, "I can't believe either of you. You're both hypocrites."

Chapter 39

BALDWIN CAN TELL I'M UPSET at school. He meets me by my locker. "What happened? Do you want to talk about it?"

"I'll tell you at lunch."

"Okay." He squeezes my hand and leaves for his first class.

In history, Conrad asks Brent if he'll trade him seats so he can sit by me. I refuse to look at him as he leans toward me. "Dandra, I need to talk to you."

I glare at him. "What if I don't want to talk to you?"

"Please?" His begging eyes break down my walls.

I cave. "Fine. Meet me under the apple tree at lunch. I'll answer your questions if you answer mine."

"Okay. That's fair enough. Just don't bring any of your new friends with you."

I feel myself bristling. "I won't."

I tell Baldwin in English that I can't meet in the library today after all. "I'm having a little chat with Conrad at lunch."

His eyes light up. "Do you want me to help you set up the recording device?"

I imagine wires going through my bra and shake my head. "No, I've got it."

"Okay. I'll be watching through the front doors. If you need me, just scratch your head, and I'll come out."

I bet my freckles are standing out with how nervous I feel. "I'll be fine. Thanks for looking out for me." He squeezes my hand briefly before anyone can see us.

When the bell rings, I go into the girl's lavatory, lock myself in a stall, and clip the microphone to my collar. I twist the knob to "on" and shove the wires and the box of the recorder into my bra. I don't think it's noticeable when I look in the mirror. Perfect.

When I walk out of the lavatory, Baldwin looks me over. I blush as his gaze lingers around my—collar. He matches steps with me and whispers, "I can't see any wires or anything. I think this is going to work."

I breathe in and out slowly as I approach the front door of

the school. I turn my face to him briefly. "Thank you, Baldwin." I can feel his eyes on my back as I walk out the door.

Conrad is already under the apple tree waiting for me with two bottles of my favorite cherry soda. "Are you thirsty?" he asks as he extends one to me. At least he had the decency to take his stupid GameCom off.

I won't be bought. "Naw, I'm fine," I say as I glare at him.

He looks hurt as he drops his arms. My traitor stomach growls just then. He hands one to me anyway. "If you don't want it, give it to Everley for me."

I take it and drop it into my jacket pocket. "Fine. Whatever."

He glares at the front doors of the school. "Do you like Baldwin Kole?"

I bite my lip as I think about how much to say. "Is this why you wanted to talk to me?"

Conrad's eyes are filled with venom. "Yes. He's no good. You have to stay away from him."

I roll my eyes. "I'm sorry that he cut the power to your dad's building. I can still be friends with him."

Conrad kicks the nearby litter in annoyance. "He wants more than friendship, Dandra."

"That's not really your concern, Conrad. You chose to lie about who killed my father, and now you have to deal with the consequences. That includes having no say in who I hang out with."

217

The silence is deafening as I feel the wires digging into my skin. I hope he says something good. He looks me in the eye, and I can see the Conrad that I've always known shrouded in a cloud of grief. He opens his mouth and each word comes out painfully. "I've never been so sorry about something in my entire life, Dandra. I chose my parents over you, and now every day is misery."

I try to choose my words wisely. "It takes a really sick parent to ask their kid to lie for them."

"I know, Dandra. They are sick. They are getting more and more unbearable to live with each day. They are so worried that someone is going to find out and that they'll lose everything."

"The truth will come out some day, Conrad. Are you going to keep lying for them?"

He reaches for my hand then drops his instead. "Will you forgive me and take me back if I tell the patrolmen my dad did it?"

He said it—and he said something that I don't know how to respond to. "I—It would change a lot of things if you did that."

"If I turn my parents in, I'll have no one but Milo left. Will you take me back?" His eyes are so sad and earnest, I don't feel sure about anything anymore.

"I can't promise that our relationship will be what you want it to be, but you would definitely be my friend again."

Conrad takes my hand. "Why does life have to be so hard?"

I look at his hand before I let it go. "Life is much easier when you tell the truth."

Conrad's eyes look frantic. "What if I lose my nerve? What if I don't want to live without my parents?"

"Then you'll just have to live without me. To be honest, if you don't tell the truth, the truth will still come out."

"What do you mean by that?"

The wires in my bra are really starting to itch, but I can't scratch myself or Baldwin will come bursting out here. "My mom has a patrolman investigating my dad's case. I guess it's up to you to decide which side of the investigation you want to be on."

"What's the patrolman's name?"

I say, "Patrolman Mark," before I can stop myself. I kick a smashed soda can in frustration. Conrad's eyes are swimming in thought. I have to protect my mom's new admirer, even if I don't like him. "If anything happens to him, I'll know who to blame."

He looks hurt. "I don't want my dad to kill anyone else, Dandra. I wish you would trust me."

That should be evidence enough for the investigation. "Prove to me that I can trust you," I say as I walk away feeling like the word Everley used to describe me this morning, a hypocrite.

Chapter 40

"I ALMOST BURST THROUGH THE DOOR ten times while you were talking to him! You were amazing," Baldwin says as we walk to the library after school. His hand reaches for mine, and I take it excitedly. I know he wants to get home to listen to my recording, but he is delaying his own desire long enough to walk me to work. I love that.

I look into the window of the ice cream shop as we pass. "Will you show me where you live? It's nearby, isn't it?"

His smile fades as he looks at me and squeezes my hand. "Not now, but I will soon." As we pause at the front door of the library, he leans forward like he's going to kiss me. My heart feels like it's going to burst out of my chest, but he just whispers in my ear, "Don't think less of me when you see where I live."

I look into his beautiful brown eyes and shake my head in disbelief. "I won't. My mom and I are barely making ends meet. I would never judge you."

His lips leave a kiss on my cheek as he ushers me into the library. "Good luck with the basement, Dandra." I hate to see him walk away. This is going to be a long day of work.

Zelma's back is to me when I approach the center desk. "Has Jed from the hardware store asked you on a date yet?"

How can I think of Jed when I can still feel Baldwin's kiss on my cheek? "No, Zelma." Her round face droops. "I went on a date with someone else though. We went stargazing."

"Ooh, that sounds romantic! Was he cute?"

I smile in spite of myself. "Yes, he was cute."

"You'll have to tell me all about it."

"Am I here to entertain you or to clean the basement?"

"Okay, fine. When you're done, you'll have to tell me about it as you walk me to the bus stop."

I roll my eyes. "Fine. Now how do I get to the basement?"

Zelma pulls out my bucket of supplies and a big key ring. She waddles to the back door of the atrium where one side of the small hallway has a male and female lavatory. The other side has a locked door that I just assumed was a closet full of dusty junk. Apparently, it is the door to the basement. Zelma unlocks it and jiggles the handle hard to get the door to open. It's so dark that I have to depend on my sense of smell to tell me that there is a lot of dust and mildew down there. When Zelma flips on the light, I can see that I'm right. The dust on this staircase is at least twice as thick as the staircase to the attic. I should have brought a sled; it looks like a snow hill. "Um, I'm getting my vacuum for this."

"Go right ahead. Whatever you need, just let me know," Zelma says as she waddles back to her desk.

I don't enjoy hauling the vacuum down from the attic, but it's worth it as the thick carpet of dust and mildew disappears off the basement staircase. Once I flip the lower light on, I see that the stairs lead to a small room with a bunch of stuff piled up around the edges in a blanket of dust. The basement has to be bigger than this. Once I have the floor dust free and the furniture unstacked and dusted, I notice a doorframe behind a skinny, sparsely-covered bookshelf.

I pull a book off the shelf and read the title: *The Art of Death*. Below the title of the book, a big red stamp reads, "Banned Book." I notice that all the books on the shelf have the same red stamp. It makes me laugh. I don't believe in banning books, but apparently Agatha does. I clean the bookshelf the same way I did all the bookshelves upstairs, but before I move the banned books back to the shelf, I shove the shelf to the right where a stack of old chairs used to be. I can't finish the basement if the door is blocked. Once the books are back on their shelves, I open the door to find an enormous room filled with all kinds of books and contraptions.

This room sends shivers down my spine more than any other that I've cleaned in this library. I walk around in awe at the collection of radios, music machines, and maps on the tables around the perimeter. My senses tell me to run back upstairs immediately. There is something very wrong with this room. It has no dust.

Chapter 41

I DON'T KNOW WHAT TO DO. Should I run upstairs and tell Zelma that someone is using the basement as a study without her knowledge? Should I wait until they come back and kick them out? Who would trespass in a public building like this? And why does it smell like the woods in here?

I wander around the gigantic room and look at the books and papers scattered on the old tables and chairs. Someone is very good at math. In an open notebook there are huge equations that I have no idea how to solve. There is a stack of books about history, chemistry, mechanics, and electricity at the largest table. A black flag with a yellow lightning bolt in the middle covers a big section of wall from floor to ceiling. That is interesting. I've never seen a flag like that before. There is a boarded-up door that looks like the six closed book rooms upstairs. It refuses to budge. As I am looking at an old music machine with a black circle in the middle, an intricately-folded piece of paper falls out of a hole in the wall onto my head.

I almost trip on a vacuum cleaner that could be a twin to the one I've been using as I pick the note up with trembling hands. There is a single letter "A" on the outside of it. I can't help myself. I open it.

A,

Meet me at the city building for the council meeting at 7:00 tonight. Bring something to record it.

Yours,

C

I look at my watch. It's 5:30. Does "C" assume that "A" is down here right now? I look around. There is no one here. They only have an hour and a half until the meeting starts. I refold the note and set it in a basket next to the music player. I look up into the hole in the wall, but it's too dark to see anything. There is a long metal pole with a claw on the end sitting nearby. I wonder if anything would come out if I used the pole to feel around in there. I notice that there are lots of holes in the walls around this room. Some are small with baskets underneath them. Some are big—big enough for a person to climb in. These holes were not made by rats. I shiver as I remember how many times I've heard scratching sounds in the walls of this library. Have people been spying on me? I feel sick to my stomach. The sick feeling continues when I spy an old, half-eaten sandwich sitting on a plate next to a pile of wires and metal. The library cleaner in me kicks in, and I pick up the sandwich to throw it away. The sandwich drops from my hand to the floor. The bread is still soft.

My breath catches in my throat and goosebumps erupt on my arms. My eyes scan the room for hiding places. Someone is in here with me. I'm sure of it. I push boxes away from the wall, look under tables, open closet doors, but I find no one. Am I losing my mind? I can't be. The bread is soft. The note was intended for someone to find before 7:00. There has to be someone here. Then I hear it. A small cough. Where did it come from? I've looked everywhere that a human being could fit. There are two locked doors, but the cough didn't come from that side of the room. I look at the huge flag one more time. It flutters slightly. I creep toward it and fling it up. Sure enough, there is a door behind it. My hand shakes as I grasp the doorknob. I really hope that the person I find isn't a rapist or a murderer.

I hurl the door open. Who I find shocks me more than a knife-wielding murderer would have. There are five scrappy-looking beds made on the floor in this tiny room with an even tinier window giving precious little light to its occupants. I know the occupants. They are Marcella, Gordon, Ed, and Adamar.

Chapter 42

I STAND THERE IN SHOCK for at least a minute, not knowing what to say. Adamar eventually clears his throat. "Did you find my sandwich?"

"Yes," I croak.

"I knew it. I shouldn't have left it out there. We panicked when we heard you in the next room over."

Ed stands up and stretches his back. He looks at Adamar and shrugs. "We tried, but the cat is out of the bag now. Can I get back to work on my microscope now?"

Adamar looks at me with worry in his eyes. "That depends,

Ed. That depends on whether Dandra is going to turn us in to the librarians upstairs."

I look at the simple beds made of old blankets and sleeping bags on the floor, the duffel bags of clothes next to them, and the box of bread and other easy-to-eat foods in the back corner. They really are homeless. But they live in the basement of the library. That is so messed up. Should I turn them in? The library has so little money that I won't be allowed to stay much longer myself. I watch Marcella hold her knees and rock back and forth as she listens to our conversation. These are my friends. I can't throw them out. They must not have anywhere else to go. "I—won't throw you out, but you have a lot of explaining to do. I thought you were my friends. Friends don't keep secrets like this from each other."

The four of them visibly sigh with relief. Gordon stands up and walks past me. "My back is killing me. Let's talk out here on some chairs."

Ed runs for the lumpy-looking old couch in the center of the room. "I call the couch."

Adamar nods. "Yeah, grab a padded seat. I can only talk for a few minutes though. I told some people that I'd meet them at the city council meeting tonight."

"You mean Charlisa?"

He looks at me curiously. "How did you know?"

I walk over to the basket and pick up the note. "This fell on my head a while ago. You're 'A' and Charlisa is 'C,' right?"

Adamar takes the note from me possessively and shoves it in his pocket. "Um, yeah. That's not supposed to be public knowledge, but I guess you're one of us now. Welcome, D."

I wish that statement made everything better, but it doesn't. "I am not one of you. I am a library employee who has been freaking out for months about the weird sounds you guys have been making down here. I can't believe you did this to me."

Adamar shifts around nervously. "It's not that we didn't want to tell you, it's just that—some of us thought it was too risky. We can't get thrown out; we have nowhere else to go."

Marcella starts moaning in her seat. I lean toward Adamar so Marcella can't hear me. "It's totally inappropriate for you boys to be living with her."

Adamar bites his lip as he watches Marcella's discomfort. "We just barely took her in a month ago. It's getting cold out there, Dandra. The only other option for a homeless girl like her is a whole lot less appropriate than staying here with us. She usually sleeps on the couch, but we tried to hide when we heard you coming."

"Why did you hide? I'm your friend."

"B—our leader-of-sorts didn't want you to find out if we could help it."

I look at the half-finished projects all around the room. "How long have you been living down here?"

Adamar scratches his chin. "Uh, the first of us have been here for six years."

My eyes bulge. "Six years! And this is the first time you've been caught?"

Adamar shakes his head. "No. This is the second time actually. We've had some close calls, especially when the boiler broke a few years ago. The people who work here are too lazy to come down into the basement."

Though I've thought the same thing many times, I hate hearing someone else criticize my coworkers. "Those lazy people are two very nice old ladies named Agatha and Zelma." I compose myself. "Who caught you the first time?"

Adamar's eyes shift back and forth. "Uh, I don't know if he'll want me to tell you that."

"Who won't want you to tell me?"

He avoids my question. "Uh, some patrolmen followed us here after we cut the power to the gaming district a year and a half ago. They broke down the emergency escape door over there and kicked us out. Luckily, we are ten times faster than your average patrolman, so most of us got away and stayed with—someone, but poor Gordon spent a few nights in the detainment center."

"Who did you stay with?"

"It doesn't matter. We only stayed a week, then we came back here. We have to use the biggest window instead of the door now that it's boarded up."

I won't be distracted. "Who did you stay with, Adamar?"

"Uh, you know, just Vern Craigstaff."

The reality of who else lives here hits me like a ton of bricks. "Where is he?"

Adamar scratches his head nervously. "Where is who? Vern?"

I feel my control breaking down. I try to keep my voice even. "I'm not an idiot. Where is Baldwin?"

Adamar laughs nervously. "He visits sometimes, but he doesn't live here."

"Adamar, it's okay. She knows," a familiar voice says from somewhere I can't see.

I stand up and walk toward the sound of his voice. "Where are you, Baldwin?"

I jump back when green sneakers appear in one of the big holes in the wall nearby. Tall, thin legs, torso, and finally all of Baldwin wiggle out of the hole in the wall.

I am amazed that he fit, yet I'm completely disgusted at the same time. He has been inches away from me in these very walls—so many times. He brushes some dust and debris off himself and steps toward me with fear in his eyes. "I—uh, told you I'd show you where I live soon."

He has been scratching the walls. He has been living under my feet all this time. I feel so betrayed. I can't hide the anger in my voice. "I told you when we went stargazing that I wanted you to be honest with me from the start."

Baldwin looks at his shoes as he nods his head.

My voice cracks with emotion. "You obviously haven't. You have no idea how creeped out I've been from your noises in the walls all these months. You should have told me. Stay away from me."

I turn and run out of the room and up the stairs.

I turn off the lights and steady myself before I face Zelma.

She smiles at me when she sees me. "You're done a bit early today. Are you ready to tell me about your date?"

"No."

Zelma looks taken back. "What's the matter? Do you feel sick?"

I hide my face behind my hand. "Yes, I feel very sick. I need to go home."

Zelma hands me some coins with a look of concern. "Get some rest, darlin'. I hope you feel better soon."

My chin quivers as I say, "Yeah. I hope so."

"By the way, did you find anything I should know about down there?"

I pause for a moment. "No, just banned books."

"Ha ha. There's no need to bring those up."

I cry as I walk the whole way home. Is there anyone I can trust anymore?

Chapter 43

MOM LOOKS AT ME WITH ALARM as I hack at the dirt at the end of the tunnel. "Did you have a bad day at work?"

"You could say that."

"What happened?"

"I—I just ran into Baldwin, and—he lied to me."

Mom purses her lips as she fills the wheelbarrow with the dirt I'm hacking out. "What did he lie about?"

"Where he lives."

Mom laughs. "Is that all? He probably just wanted to impress you."

I think about that for a minute. "Yeah, but I specifically

told him how much Conrad's lies hurt me, and I asked him not to lie to me ever. He obviously doesn't care how I feel."

Mom looks around at the ever-expanding tunnel. "People make mistakes, Dandra. If you give up on every person who has made a mistake, you will find yourself all alone one day."

I sneeze and wipe my nose on the back of my hand. "You and Everley are the only people I can trust anymore."

"We make mistakes too, you know."

I pick up Mom's abandoned shovel and hand it back to her. "Mom, the people in this country are far worse than Dad thought. We need to get out as soon as possible."

Mom lifts her shovel then sets it back down. "I want out too, Dandra, but don't let this tunnel be an excuse not to resolve things with your friends."

"Friends? I thought we were talking about Baldwin."

"We are, but I think Baldwin's lie wouldn't have hurt so much if you hadn't been licking your wounds from Conrad when it happened."

"I recorded Conrad saying that Zane killed Dad today, Mom. I'm turning his whole family in. I can't 'resolve' things with him. We're done."

Mom's face looks conflicted. "Okay, if you say so." She brushes some dirt off of her clothes. "Mark has been giving me daily updates on his investigation of the Chestertons. I'll tell him that you have something for him."

"Speaking of Mark, why did he send you flowers?"

Mom looks at me hesitantly. "I—I'm dating him, Dandra."

I can't take any more. I drop my shovel on the ground and march out of the tunnel without a backward glance.

Chapter 44

EVERLEY LECTURES ME THE WHOLE WAY
to school. "You are the worst sister in the world. You cry and
scowl all the time. You never smile. You work late almost
every day. You won't let me talk to Conrad. You never take me
anywhere fun anymore. I wish I could have my old sister back."

I feel a tear trying to escape my eye as I say, "I wish you
could have your old sister back, too."

Everley is quiet as she looks at my face. "I'm sorry, Dandra.
You aren't the worst sister in the world."

This confession means more than she knows. I stop

and hug her until she starts to squirm. "I'm sorry I've been so gloomy lately. Let's do something fun together this weekend."

"Okay! Can I invite Conrad?"

"No."

Everley frowns. "I miss him."

"I know." I give Everley one last hug as I drop her off at the low-level school. Conrad and Baldwin's betrayals were so hard-fixed in my mind last night, but I realize now that my angry feelings aren't hurting them as much as they're hurting me.

I decide to ease up a notch as I walk into school. Charlisa walks me to my first class. "I know you are angry, Dandra, but it isn't their fault that their parents left them homeless. They should be menaces to society after everything they've been through, but they're not. Remember that. They are probably the smartest students in our school even though they have no support."

"They steal to live, Charlisa. My dad told me about them."

Charlisa's face is blank. "I won't say that they haven't stolen anything, but that's not how they live. They scavenge and they work, just like you do."

"I just wish intelligence and honesty could come in the same package these days," I say with a flat voice.

Charlisa sighs. "Baldwin is so embarrassed and ashamed, Dandra. Be kind to him and let him explain himself."

The tension in my limbs refuses to let go. "I'll try, Charlisa, but I can't take much more drama."

"You won't regret it," she says as she nudges me with her shoulder.

History is miserable because Conrad doesn't sit by me, yet he keeps looking at me across the room. I try to pretend like Molly's brainless chatter is funny and meaningful during group discussions, but I have to admit, I'd love to hear two words of sense spoken together right about now, even if it is from Conrad.

English is even worse. Baldwin makes Wendy move so he can sit by me. I turn away so I don't have to look at his eyes.

He touches my arm gently. "Dandra, I know you asked me not lie to you, but I was afraid. I've worked so hard to earn people's respect in the academic world, and I didn't think you, or anyone in your world for that matter, would give me a chance if you knew that I have absolutely nothing.

My head snaps around to face him. "I knew you were homeless, Baldwin. I was just waiting for you to admit it to me. You may think you have nothing, but brains and truth are two things that I value higher than anything else, and they don't cost a cent."

Baldwin's eyes freeze in place. "I'm so sorry. I was afraid. More afraid than when I was on the run from my dad. I want you to see me as more than a homeless kid."

"I do, but you can't lie to me."

"I won't lie to you ever again."

"Dandra and Baldwin, do you want to share with the class

what you find so important to talk about while I'm teaching?"
Mrs. Jones asks.

Baldwin gives her one of his dazzling smiles and says, "We
were just discussing how the word "foil" in this passage doesn't
mean the shiny stuff people wrap their leftover food in, but
means that the rude brother has exactly opposite character traits
from the groom at the wedding."

Mrs. Jones frowns. "Yes, that is easily missed. Keep your
eyes forward, please."

Baldwin passes a note to me when Mrs. Jones is writing
something on the board.

D,

*I'll explain everything after school in the crypt, aka the
basement of the library, if you want to hear it. I hope you do.*

B

I crumble the note into a ball and shove it in my pocket.
He called me "D." Despite my anger at being lied to, it makes me
smile inside.

Chapter 45

I FEEL A LITTLE BIT GUILTY when I tell Agatha that I should have the basement finished by tonight. It's already dust-free. Maybe I can just help the boys and Marcella organize their stuff and scrub any dirty places as we talk.

I don't know what to expect as I slip down the stairs and enter "the crypt."

Baldwin meets me at the door by the banned books and ushers me in. It seems like he wants to take my hand, but he's afraid to. "Here, sit in this chair. This is the most comfortable one that we have," he says hesitantly.

I sit stiffly in the oversized leather chair offered to me. Ed is helping Marcella with her math homework at a big table close by, Gordon is working on the telescope we used when we went stargazing, and Adamar is sitting next to Baldwin on the ugly, lumpy couch. His grin is infuriating.

"I'm being paid to clean this basement, so make this quick," I say as Baldwin looks at me apprehensively.

Baldwin shakes his head. "I know that this basement is gross to you, but you don't have to clean anything. We'll do it."

"I should hope so. This is not a normal place to live, Baldwin."

His eyes are full of pain. "I know, but it is a whole lot better than an old car in a junk yard."

I choke on my words. "Is that—where you lived before this?"

Baldwin rubs his hands on the legs of his pants. I've never seen him show a lack of confidence like this. "Yeah. My mom died when I was six, and my dad became a drunk—not a harmless drunk like Vern Craigstaff, who did occasionally drink with him—but a mean, abusive drunk." I cringe as I think about that kind of home life. Baldwin goes on, "When I was ten, my dad punched me in the face so hard I was knocked out for over a day. When I woke up, he was gone to work, and there was no food except a can of beans in the house. I packed my bag and left." He looks down at his green sneakers. "I ate out of garbage cans and slept in a big old boat of a car in the junk yard until it started snowing."

I can't even imagine it. "Did your dad come after you?"

"Vern said he looked for me for a couple of weeks, but then he gave up. He never reported me as a runaway either. He drank himself to death two years later."

The cold feelings in my heart melt away. "That is terrible." I look around at the somewhat homey-looking room I'm in. "How did you find a way into this basement? They keep it locked."

Baldwin nods. "If I wasn't at school, I was here, at the library, reading until closing time. It was a safe, warm place to stay until dark. When Agatha or Zelma kicked me out each night, I dreaded the hours in the car until school started the next day."

"So you just snooped around until you found a way into the basement? Did you come through one of these big holes in the wall?"

Adamar laughs. "No. We made those holes to get into the locked book rooms last year."

Baldwin claps his friend on the shoulder. "You remember the day we found the crypt, don't you?" Adamar nods and snorts. Baldwin looks at the boarded-up window in the corner of the room. "One night, Agatha sent me out at closing time, and as I was walking away, I heard glass breaking from the back of the library. I ran around to the back and found Adamar trying to get through that window right there." He points to the window in question. "I tried to stop him, but he disappeared into the basement, so I followed him."

I try to imagine what ten-year-old Baldwin and Adamar must have looked like.

"We just sat there in the dust and broken glass for a while, wondering if we were going to get caught," Adamar says with a snicker.

"Adamar wanted to steal anything that would fetch a price and get back to his hut under the Crinkton Bridge, but I saw the door over there, and the old furniture piled up in here as potential for warmth and shelter. I really didn't want to spend the winter in that old car," Baldwin recounts.

Adamar grins. "I remember looking at you and saying, 'What are you thinking? I may have nothing, but I'm not staying in this dusty old crypt.' I guess the name stuck."

Baldwin smiles. "Yeah, the crypt became home that day. I fixed the old vacuum cleaner over there and made this basement fit for habitation."

I look around. "But what about showers and toilets?"

Baldwin shrugs. "There is a janitorial closet in the boiler room. We just use the hose and drain to clean ourselves, and there is a tiny unfinished lavatory over there that has a toilet and a sink. We locked it when we heard you coming yesterday, but we have hot water, so it's just fine."

I look around the basement with doubts obscuring my vision of its potential. "Oh, good. Show me."

Baldwin leads me to the rooms in question and doesn't seem to think there is a problem with the inch of grime on everything. It kind of breaks my heart. I've never appreciated my mom and my house as much as I do in this moment.

I roll up my sleeves. "I'll start cleaning in here."

Baldwin blocks me from the dirty sink. "No, you won't. If anyone is going to clean this, it will be the people who dirtied it." He calls out the door of the lavatory, "Adamar, Gordon, everybody, get the cleaning supplies Dandra left down here yesterday, and help me clean all the water rooms."

They all grumble and complain, but surprisingly, they stand up and get to work. I look at Baldwin in awe as he starts cleaning the toilet. "How did you get them to work so easily? I never see teenagers working anymore—well, besides me."

Baldwin doesn't answer me until he has finished cleaning the toilet. "We aren't your average teenagers."

"I can imagine. How did you all find each other?"

"Well, Adamar lived under a bridge and stole for a living until he found me six years ago. It was just the two of us for a while. A few years ago, I stopped Ed's brother from killing him because he ate their last can of food. He was happy to join us." Baldwin takes a rag and scrubs some dirty spots off the walls. "I found Gordon skeletal and drug-dazed in a gutter a year later, and I paid Marcella's pimp to free her from her contract a month ago. I guess you could say that they feel like they owe me, so they listen to me."

247

The shock I feel must be showing on my face because Baldwin gently closes my jaw with his finger. My voice cracks as I say, "You are some kind of miracle worker." I imagine the people these guys left behind. "Don't ghosts from your pasts ever haunt you?"

Balwin's eyes look sad. "Yeah, they do. We have to hide our money from Gordon when his old friends start pestering him to party with them again. Marcella doesn't talk about her past, but she wakes up screaming every other night. When I keep them focused on our cause, their issues seem to lessen. Reading and learning saved me; it's saving them now, too."

Marcella knocks on the lavatory door and peeks her head in. "All done, B," she says as she drops a bucket of cleaning supplies at Baldwin's feet.

"Thank you," he says as he grabs some soap and a scrub brush out of the bucket and attacks the sink. He may not have as much practice as me, but the sink looks much better when he's done.

After he washes his hands in the newly-cleaned sink, I pull him over to me and give him a hug. I expect him to let go, but he doesn't for a long time. He pushes a stray piece of my straggly blonde hair behind my ear. "Does this mean that you forgive me?"

I let him go and put my hands into my pockets. "Yeah. I see how much you have to lose if you get kicked out of here. You can trust me." I take his hand in mine. "But I want to completely trust you too. No more secrets." Baldwin nods his head sheepishly. I continue, "Remember when you told me that you'd rather know the awfulness of the truth than be happy in ignorance? That's how we both want it. Can we handle that?"

He pulls me closer and lifts my chin up. "Yes." There is nothing more to say because our lips have found something else to do.

Chapter 46

I WISH OUR KISS COULD LAST FOREVER, but
of course, it can't. *Bam, bam, bam.* "Baldwin, what are you
doing in there? Ernestine is trying to contact you on the radio,"
Gordon calls out.

Baldwin pulls me out of the lavatory faster than Adamar
can make a cookie disappear. "Tell her I'm coming!" He kisses
me on the forehead and drags me to the couch. "I've been
waiting for this call for days. My radio isn't very clear, so this is
going to take all of my concentration. Will you be okay for a bit
without me?"

My eyebrows almost touch as I watch his excitement. "Sure. Just don't take too long."

"I won't." He squeezes my hand and then runs to the far corner of the room with all the radio equipment.

I look at Marcella and Ed, who are looking at me distrustfully. This is awkward. I need to find something to talk to them about. "Where have all these things come from?" I ask as I motion to the academic items around the room.

Ed shrugs. "Most of them were already down here."

He avoids my gaze after that, but I won't be deterred. "Where did the rest of them come from?"

"They uh, were acquired."

I press harder. "Were they stolen?"

Ed licks his lips nervously. "B doesn't allow us to steal anything, but we can take stuff from the garbage and free things if we want."

Marcella pipes in, "We all stole things before we came here. It's hard to eat on the street otherwise."

I motion with my hand around the enormous room. "How much of this is stolen do you think?"

She shrugs, but Ed says, "Just the radio, the fridge, the atlas, the soldering iron, and the flag."

I shake my head in disgust. "Why the flag?"

"Because it pissed Zane Chesterton off more than when we cut his power. It's some kind of symbol for gamers or something."

I can't help but laugh. "You are terrible."

"Not as terrible as he is. I'm so glad that you got Conrad's confession. I took it to Patrolman Mark before school this morning."

This surprises me. "Thank you, but you didn't have to do that. I was going to take it to him."

Ed waves his hand like it was nothing. "Oh, I don't mind. Patrolman Mark always makes the trouble worth my time."

My eyes pop. "Is that your job? Are you an informant?"

"Yep."

I raise my eyebrows. "Well, at least it's for a good patrolman. What do the rest of you do?"

Marcella looks at me sheepishly. "I just got a job at the bakery in the Food Mart. I get an employee discount, and I can take home any mess-ups."

Ed looks at Gordon as he fiddles with the telescope. "Gordon is a janitor at the high-level school. Adamar is janitor in the mayor's office, and Baldwin is a landscaper."

That last job is surprising. "A landscaper? Does anyone care about their lawns anymore in Tifton?"

Ed shrugs. "Not really. He mainly pulls weeds and mows lawns for higher-end businesses, like the gaming district, restaurants, and the autobody shop, for example."

I imagine Baldwin pulling weeds with his eyes and ears wide open. "Oh. It makes sense how you guys have so much information now."

Baldwin comes around the corner and plops down on the couch next to me. He puts his arm around my shoulders and says excitedly, "I have good news. If we can find a way across the border wall, Ernestine will help us start over in the United Cities."

Adamar looks less than enthusiastic as he puts on his jacket and grabs a notebook. "That sounds great and all but think of all the people we'd have to leave behind." I think we all know who he's talking about. Charlisa can't leave her mother very easily.

Ed snickers. "What's the point of even thinking about it? There is no way to cross that border wall—unless we find a hidden stock of dynamite—and we all know it."

I find myself squirming in my seat. Do I tell them? They just spilled a lot of secrets to me—and Baldwin and I agreed to tell each other the absolute truth from here on out.

Baldwin looks at me like he can read my mind. "Do you have something you want to say, Dandra?"

Here goes nothing. "Yes, I do. I know how to get under the border wall into the United Cities."

Chapter 47

I TELL AGATHA that only the porcelain in the basement got cleaned today, and that I haven't been feeling well, so I spent most of my time recuperating on the old couch in the basement, so I don't want her to pay me very much.

"You are too modest. This library is sparkling from top to bottom now because of you. Just let me pay you the full amount." She slides a stack of coins toward me.

I take half of the coins and slide them back. "No, I couldn't."

Agatha slides them back to me and walks away. "Too bad. Spend it on your sister and get some rest." Why does everyone like to play the sister card on me? Because it works.

I don't know what else I can say without giving anything away, so I just take the coins. "Thank you."

"Remind your mom to vote tomorrow."

"Why?"

"Do you want to be done with school?"

"No."

"Well, you will be if you don't find more people like your mom to vote against the amendment tomorrow."

I feel my heart sink into my feet. "I completely forgot about the vote."

I AM AMAZED AS I TRY to walk into school the next day. There is a crowd of adults at the front doors of the school waiting to vote, and I can barely squeeze past them to get into the building. They look like they woke up earlier than they are used to as they rub the sleep out of their eyes. I feel like I should say something to them since I haven't done anything else to help education in my country. I am my dad's daughter after all. I have to say something. Once I'm in the school, I turn to the line and say, "Thank you for wanting to support your children's education. Vote no on the educational amendment."

The crowd of people look at me silently for a few seconds, and then they start laughing. Not just a little chuckle—30 adults full-belly laugh at me. If that doesn't hurt enough, seeing

Conrad's parents in the middle of the group laughing with them sends me moping with my head down into my first class.

I am still hiding my eyes from the world when second-hour history begins. Conrad sits by me, which is surprising. I can feel his eyes on me for a long time, and I finally cave in and look at him. "What do you want, Conrad?"

"I want to know what's wrong. You look terrible. Is it Baldwin?"

"No, it's your parents and 30 other people who just laughed at me when I said we should keep going to school."

Conrad looks like I just slapped him in the face. "I told them that I want to keep going to school. I told them that I will be the dumb one of the family if I don't keep going."

"What did they say?"

"They said I would keep going no matter what, but the rest of my grade are ready to join the working gamers."

I look at the GameCom on Conrad's arm and sigh. "You can't live with one foot on each side of the line forever, you know."

I seem to have hit a nerve. He sits up straighter. "I know." He looks down at his GameCom. "My whole family has been summoned for questioning tonight at 5:00. I think this has something to do with your pal, Patrolman Mark."

I search his eyes. "What are you going to say, Conrad?"

"I don't know yet."

I feel a tear leak out of the corner of my eye. I can't tell if the tear is for my dad, who is dead; Vern, who is locked up for someone else's crime; or—Conrad. I wish I could help him get through this thing at 5:00.

I look at him with all the sympathy that I can muster. "I—can't imagine how hard this is going to be for you." I want to touch his hand, but I don't.

"Yeah. It's hard to think about anything else." I notice his eye twitching.

I lean toward him. "I hope you find the strength to tell the truth. It could make your life—so hard, but I will be there for you if you do the right thing."

"I wish you would be there for me no matter what," Conrad says dejectedly.

My eyebrows crease together. "This isn't just about us. This is about justice and a lot of people, some of whom are suffering in a detainment center right now."

"I know."

I lean closer to him and whisper, "Your lies have hurt me so much, Conrad, and I know your dad forced a fake friendship on us, but I still liked being your friend, and I—believe in you."

His eyes look achingly into mine. "Thank you." The urge to hold his hand overwhelms me again, but I don't do it.

Chapter 48

BALDWIN CAN TELL that something is bothering me in English class. "I heard about the voters laughing at you. I'm sorry. Those guys aren't all the voters though. The amendment still might not pass."

"It's not that."

"What is it then?"

"Conrad is going in for questioning today."

Baldwin claps his hands together. "Good. The recording has him cornered. He'll have to tell the truth."

My eyes feel heavy. "Yeah. And he'll lose his parents."

"Oh," Baldwin says with realization.

I fake a smile as I look at the split ends in my hair. "I don't think he wants to join you in the crypt."

"No, I don't think he'd move in with me if I were the last human being alive."

"Yeah."

THE VOTING ENDS right before school gets out. I wonder if my mom and the other working parents had a chance to vote. The small window for voting seems incredibly unfair. Since the library is clean from top to bottom, I don't feel bad for staying late at the school to hear the results of the vote. I'm not the only one. All of the upper-classmen of the school wait with me. Charlisa stands by me until her mom shows up and insists that she stand by her.

Conrad is just a few people to the right. He keeps glancing my way until Baldwin surprises me by putting his arm around me before I know he's there. Conrad brushes past us roughly on his way out, muttering about getting to the detainment center on time.

"Are you okay?" Baldwin asks into my hair.

"Uh, yeah. I'm fine." But really, my stomach is queasy.

Mr. Henry comes out of the office with a paper in his hand. "May I have your attention? We have the results of the educational amendment vote. With 90% of the vote, the educational amendment—passes. All students age 16 and up are no longer required to attend middle-level school. If any of you wish to withdraw from school at this time, please line up in front of the office to be checked out."

The crowd around me parts and forms a line that spills out of the building in a matter of minutes. Baldwin and I just stand there and watch their happy faces in disappointment.

I DON'T HAVE THE HEART to go to work. Baldwin says he won't go to work either. So he walks me home. Everley squeals with delight when I open the front door. "Yay! I can't believe you skipped work today!" When she sees Baldwin with me, the smile slides right off her face. "What is he doing here?"

"Everley, this is Baldwin; he is my boyfriend."

My sister's eyes flicker with fire. "Whatever," she says as she stomps upstairs.

Baldwin's face caves. "What did I do?"

I give his shoulder a squeeze. "Nothing. She just misses Conrad."

He frowns. "Oh." Baldwin looks around the house as I pull out a couple of apples for a snack. His face doesn't give away how he feels about where I live as he eats his apple. When he's finished, he asks, "Is there any chance I can see your dad's tunnel?"

I swallow a bite and say, "Yeah, sure. Follow me."

We walk out back together, and I giggle at Baldwin's confusion when we enter the shed.

He frowns and looks around until I lift up the board on the floor. I love the way his eyes pop out of his head. "This is the perfect place to start a tunnel. Your dad was a genius."

"I know. Wait until you see inside it."

Baldwin's mouth hangs open when I show him how far the tunnel goes. He pulls a tape measure and a sheet of paper out of his backpack and writes down how far we've come and how far we have to go. He asks how much progress we make per day and forms an equation on how long it will take to finish the tunnel. He really is a doer. "It will take you and your mom nine months to finish the tunnel at the rate you're going."

"Huh. That sounds about right."

Baldwin bounces on the balls of his feet. "Is there any way you will let us help you? It would speed things along."

I look at the blisters on my hands and start picking at them. "Uh, I don't have a problem with that, but my mom might."

Baldwin puts both hands on my shoulders, his eyes full of excitement. "Will you talk to her about it? We could be out of here in a month if we work around the clock."

He's so excited, I don't want to burst his bubble. "Uh, yeah. Sure."

"Thanks, Dandra," he says as he kisses me on the forehead. "I'll tell Ernestine to be ready for us the day after Christmas."

Whoa, this just got real. I hope my mom will be okay with this. I fake a smile. "Yeah. Perfect."

Chapter 49

EVERLEY GLARES AT ME when I walk back into the house. "I listened to you two talking just now. I was in the shed listening from the top of the tunnel."

I growl at her. "How would you like it if I did the same thing to you?"

"I don't care, because I don't have anything I want to hide from you. Why are you going to let him use our tunnel? I don't want to leave with him. I want to leave with Conrad."

Anger fills my veins. "That's nice, sis, but I don't think Conrad wants to leave with us."

"But what if he does?" She folds her arms across her chest and taps her foot waiting for a reply.

I roll my eyes. "Then he can come with us, I guess."

She smiles with righteous indignation. "Good."

I glare at her. "He won't want to come."

Mom bursts through the door as Everley stomps away from me. "Why aren't you at work, Dandra?"

I look at the back door where Baldwin was not too long ago. "I wanted to hear how the vote turned out."

Mom throws her hands up in the air. "Yes, that is terrible. I barely made it back to work on time when I voted during my lunch break. They should have made the voting hours longer for those who work."

"Do you think they made the hours short on purpose?"

"Yes, I do." Mom plops down in a kitchen chair. "We are all going to feel the effects of this sooner than later."

I frown. "I know. You should have seen the line of kids checking out of school."

Mom sits up straighter and takes off her coat. "Just so you know, Patrolman Mark will be here in half an hour. He says he has important news for us."

I watch my mom buzz around the kitchen trying to make it and herself look nice. I clear my throat. "I'm pretty sure I know what it is about. He called Conrad's family in for questioning."

Mom stops in her tracks. "Do you have any idea how Conrad is going to answer those questions?"

I remember our conversation in History class earlier, but I also remember him brushing past Baldwin and I tonight after school. "I have no idea, Mom."

Chapter 50

KNOCK, KNOCK. EVERLEY OPENS THE DOOR at Mom's prompting. She has a fixed scowl on her face, much to Mom's dismay. Patrolman Mark seems unsure of himself as he walks through the door. He hesitantly takes Mom's hand and says, "I wish I came with good news."

My eyebrows come together in frustration. "You have a confession. How can there be bad news?"

Mark sighs. "I don't know how to tell you this, so I'll just say it. Once Conrad listened to the tape you gave us, he admitted to lying to us. He said his dad ran over Gifford and has been working hard to keep the truth hidden ever since."

I hug my mom. "He did it! This is great news."

Mark rubs his forehead. "Well, I thought so until I told Zane what his son had done. He says that his son is mentally unstable and needs professional help. I played the tape for him, and he says that Conrad has been mentally unstable for months. He says Dandra used her womanly influences to trick his son into saying those things."

I throw my hands in the air. "That is ridiculous."

Mark nods. "I know that, but my superior isn't so sure. He going to start an investigation of his own."

Mom leans forward. "Don't you suspect him of being on Zane Chesterton's payroll?"

Mark sighs. "Yes, I do. I'm worried that things might get worse for you instead of better."

I sink into a chair. "Oh, no."

Mark lowers his voice. "Be very careful what you say and who you say it to. You are all going to be watched starting tomorrow."

I crumple into a sprawling mess on the table. I look up from my arms. "Is there anything we can do? I feel like Zane owns everyone. Is there someone above your boss who can help us?"

Mark rubs his chin. "Maybe. I'll try my best."

I force a smile at my mom's boyfriend. "Thank you. I know I haven't been very friendly to you, but I don't know what we'd do without you."

Mark's ears turn red. "Oh, well, you're welcome."

Mom takes Mark's arm and gives him a winning smile. "Would you like to stay for a slice of pie?"

He looks at Everley and me with apprehension. "Sure."

Everley stomps out of the room.

I DON'T SLEEP. HOW CAN I? Conrad did the right thing, and now his dad is throwing him under the bus to protect himself. It's disgusting. Baldwin wants to work on the tunnel around the clock, but we're going to be watched. Just when I think things can't get worse, they do.

My eyes have huge bags under them when I get to school, but it doesn't matter, because hardly anyone is there. Adamar and I are the only people in my first-hour math class. Mr. Jin is particularly jumpy as he teaches the two of us. When the bell rings, I ask him if he's okay. He says, "If there are only two students in each of my classes, they will cut most of them, and only getting pay for one or two classes instead of four or five isn't going to give me enough to live on."

That sounds incredibly familiar.

My history class has only two students as well. Well, two students and one mental health professional. I wish Conrad and I could talk since we're the only two left in the class, but Mrs. Graight, Conrad's "psychologist," won't let us sit within 10 feet of each other. When it's time for group work, Mrs. Graight writes down everything we say, so we stay ridiculously on topic.

When she's writing something down in her notes, I mouth the words, "I'm so sorry," to him. He nods, but his eyes are dead. What has Zane done to him?

Third hour English is a huge class with four students in it. Baldwin, Ed, Marcella, and I commiserate with Mrs. Jones, who is also worried about losing her job. "I can try to get some younger classes, I suppose. I don't know what else I can do." I smile at her sympathetically. What is this world coming to?

An announcement comes over the loud speakers. "All students age 16 and up need to come to the office for required class schedule changes immediately. All teachers stay in your usual classes for today, but your schedules will change tomorrow."

There are a whopping 20 students out of the original 200 upperclassmen standing in line with me at the office. Baldwin takes my hand and whispers into my ear, "Who is that woman with Conrad?"

I whisper back, "Things didn't go well during his interrogation yesterday. He told Patrolman Mark the truth, but his dad says he's mentally unstable, so now he has a psychologist following him everywhere. It's terrible." I can see Conrad's sad eyes watching me from the back of the line.

Baldwin is watching Conrad too. He leans forward and kisses me, which causes Conrad to stalk off toward the lavatory.

Mrs. Graight chases after him. He turns as he enters the men's lavatory and yells, "I can at least be alone when I relieve myself, right?"

She turns red and walks back to the line.

Baldwin snickers. "Maybe he's more mentally disturbed than you think."

I glare at him. "That's not funny. He is being punished for doing the right thing."

"Sorry," he says abashedly.

I sigh and whisper, "Patrolman Mark says we're being watched by people on Zane's payroll. I don't know if we can dig around the clock after all."

Baldwin shrugs. "You'll just have to lead them away, so we can dig."

"The only time I'm away is during school and when I'm working at the library."

Baldwin's eyes are calculating. "I can work with that. It looks like you're next."

The secretary smiles at me as I approach her desk. "Dandra Metty, it looks like you are the lucky one. Your schedule won't change at all, but all of the remaining students your age will have the same schedule as you."

"How many students is that exactly?"

"Nine."

There are only nine of us left. "I'll have the same nine students in each of my classes now. Is that correct?"

"Yes. I'm sure you'll all become the best of friends."

I look behind me at the line with mostly anti-gamers and Conrad left. "Sure."

I can't imagine having Baldwin and Conrad in every class with me. It is going to be so awkward. I hope Baldwin can figure out a way to finish the tunnel, even with all of us being watched.

Chapter 51

AS I LEAVE SCHOOL, there are many of our old classmates standing around the school grounds with GameComs on their arms laughing at us. Baldwin puts his arm around me as we walk through the crowd. Philip bumps Baldwin with his arm. "Just so you know, the gaming district is selling these on credit now. I'll have mine paid off in a year. You should get one."

"No thanks, man."

"What's wrong with you, anyway? Why are you still going to school when you don't have to?"

"I want to."

"Whatever."

Baldwin walks me to the library in silence. "I am going to work on the tunnel while you're at the library today, okay?"

"Okay. What about your job?"

"There isn't much to do now that it's cold. I'm only working twice a week."

"You'll have to be ghostlike. I haven't exactly told my mom our plans yet, and our house is probably being watched."

"I'm good at ghostlike; you thought I was a rat in the library walls, remember? Don't worry about me. I'll see you later."

He kisses me quickly and takes off for my house.

I am lost in thought as I enter the library. Agatha startles me when she meets me in the entryway. "Dandra, I'm so glad to see you. I missed you yesterday."

"I'm sorry, I wanted to see how the vote turned out."

"Yeah, I figured as much. Look at what arrived today!" She shows me new black letters that spell "Library" in her hands. "I want the outside to look as nice as the inside. Will you nail these on for me?"

"Yes, absolutely."

"Wonderful. Then you can start dusting the third floor again."

"Sure thing. When are you meeting with the mayor?"

"Tomorrow."

"Oh. Good timing for the letters then."

276

"Yes, let's hope so."

The new letters nail on nicely and look great above the door. I feel happy as I head up the stairs to dust the third floor. I only have one shelf done when a patrolman interrupts me. "Excuse me, are you Dandra Metty?"

"Yes, I am."

"I am Patrolman Darius. I need to ask you a few questions about your father's death and your relationship with Conrad Chesterton."

"Okay." He asks me a lot of questions that I feel like I've answered before, until he gets to the subject of Conrad.

"What is your relationship with Conrad Chesterton?"

"Well, we used to be best friends, but now our relationship is strained."

"Is it strained because he likes you more than you like him?"

"No, well, yes, but mostly no. He admitted that he likes me more than I like him, but he also admitted that he lied about who killed my dad to cover his own dad's tracks. That is why our relationship is strained."

"Are you sure that he said that of his own free will? Or did you let your own assumptions paint a new picture of what happened in that poor, lovesick boy's mind?"

What a biased jerk. "I am sure that Conrad lied to me for a long time and finally told me the truth. He is mentally stable and being used by his father. You need to stop looking at Conrad and start looking at Zane."

"You are too biased to give accurate advice in this investigation."

"At least I know that the money I earn isn't from bribes," I say as I storm down the stairs.

Chapter 52

I HIDE IN THE LAVATORY until I'm sure Darius is gone. I hope I don't regret my outburst. I dust the third floor with fiery rage. At least my problems are helping me make the library nicer for the mayor tomorrow. I cross paths with Baldwin on the way home. I reach for his hands. "Did any patrolmen see you?"

He sighs. "Not coming out of your yard, but there is a mean-looking patrolman that just pulled up to the curb around the corner."

I give him a quick kiss. "Don't do anything suspicious if

you see someone watching. I better get home. He knows the library is closed now."

He whispers into my hair, "See you at school tomorrow."

"Bye."

The man in the patrol car is definitely Patrolman Darius. I slip into my house without a backward glance.

Mom is trying to salvage some burned bacon. "I can't believe I burned it! I was splurging when I bought it in the first place. What a waste of money!"

"It's fine, Mom," I say as I pop a blackened piece into my mouth. "I like it on the well-done side." The slight cringe on my face doesn't fool my mom.

"You are so nice. Did you have a good day at school and work?"

I sigh. "Nope. Everywhere I go these days is rather lonely."

Knock, knock.

Mom pulls her bacon-scented apron off and throws it in the open lavatory door. "I bet it's Patrolman Darius. He questioned me at work and now he's watching our house."

I open my eyes wide at my grouchy sister across the table. "Everyone act natural and don't say anything if you can help it."

Mom opens the door without asking anyone to come in. "Hello. May I help you?"

Patrolman Darius walks into the house, farther inside than is customary, and starts poking around. "Mrs. Metty, I need to ask you a few questions about your husband's death."

"I have told your office everything that I know."

He picks a dead leaf off our geranium plant. "Did Zane Chesterton give you food for your husband's funeral?"

Mom pours a cup of water for the plant. "Yes."

He touches my Dad's old clock on the mantle. "Did you accept the food offered?"

Mom gives the dying plant a drink. "Yes."

"Why would he do that if he had just killed your husband?"

Mom's eyebrows come together. "I'm sure it was to cover his tracks."

Patrolman Darius looks annoyed. "That sounds like someone trying to be a good neighbor to me."

I glare at him. "Is he a good neighbor to you?"

Darius smirks. "As a matter of fact, yes."

Mom stands as tall as she can. "I know what you're doing here, and who is paying for it. You should care more about justice."

"I am justice in this town," he says and turns to leave.

Chapter 53

MOM PULLS MY ARM. "Come out to the shed with me, Dandra."

She's going to see what Baldwin dug out tonight. I smile at her. "Yeah, I've been meaning to talk to you about that."

She lowers her voice. "About what?"

I smile awkwardly. "Just follow me. Hey, Everley, we'll be out in the shed if you need us."

She rolls her eyes at me and looks for something not burned to eat.

When we get to the shed, my mom is shocked at how much dirt is dug out and gone. Baldwin must have hauled the loose dirt to the truck. "How did this happen? Did you skip school?"

"No, Mom. I told Baldwin about it. He dug all of this out."

Mom stops in her tracks. "What? Are you crazy?"

I shake my head. "No, I'm not crazy. He wants to get out of here too. He has a friend he talks to over radios in the United Cities."

"Whoa. You should have told me this before letting him in here."

I start playing with the end of my blonde ponytail. "I'm sorry. I just think we can use some help. Many hands make light work."

Mom closes her eyes in frustration. "How many people know about this?"

"Just six."

"Dandra, we're being watched! It only takes one set of lips to ruin everything."

I scratch my arm nervously. "What can I do about it now?"

"Hope we don't get sent to the detainment center."

Chapter 54

CLASS WITH THE SAME NINE PEOPLE isn't terrible, but it's definitely awkward because of Conrad. Mrs. Graight refuses to let him sit by me, and he is looking worse and worse all the time. I wish I could ask him about it. The opportunity presents itself during third hour. Mrs. Graight stands up and runs out of the room right as we're divided into two groups for discussion.

Ed laughs loud enough that we all turn to look at him. "Uh, I think she needs to use the lavatory."

I wait until Mrs. Jones peeks out the window of the door after her. "Why do you think that?"

Ed's eyes start to water he's laughing so hard. "Because I might have slipped some laxative into her coffee."

Conrad's unused voice croaks, "Why would you do that?"

Ed wipes the tears from his eyes. "I'm tired of her watching me."

Conrad frowns. "She isn't watching you; she's watching me."

Ed smirks. "I know. You're welcome."

Mrs. Jones shakes her head. "I should turn you in, but I don't like her in here any more than you do, so I'm going to let this one slide."

Ed slaps his desk. "You're the best!"

"I know, now get into your groups and discuss this story. Dandra and Baldwin, I want you two in separate groups this time." Baldwin smiles at me and shrugs.

Conrad scoots closer to Ed. "Hey, do you have any more of those laxatives on you?"

He shrugs. "I do for five coins per dose."

"Deal." Conrad slaps a handful of coins into Ed's palm as Mrs. Jones writes on the board. He pockets the pills and scoots closer to me.

I hope I don't regret this. I lean toward him. "What is going on with you? You look like death." Mrs. Jones clears her throat as she hands the two of us a worksheet.

His sleep-deprived eyes look at me longingly. "Well, someone recorded me admitting that my dad is guilty, so I told the patrolmen everything. My dad didn't like that, so I'm spending my days attached to my babysitter's hip." I notice that he writes "RadOak16" instead of his name on the worksheet. I'm guessing it's a nickname he wants to adopt or something.

I feel like scum. "I'm sorry, Conrad. I was trying to—"

He shrugs. "I know. I forgive you."

Wow. He makes forgiveness seem—easy. I smile at him. "You know, I bet Mrs. Jones would appreciate your real name."

"Oh, yeah. I forgot I'm here." He erases his weird nickname and writes "Conrad Chesterton" instead.

I pat his hand. "Isn't she only following you at school?"

He smiles humorlessly. "No, she follows me at home too. I think my dad is starting to believe his own lies."

"I can't believe it."

Mrs. Graight comes back to the classroom looking a little bit worse for wear. Conrad turns away from me for the rest of the class.

Chapter 55

"I DON'T WANT TO GO to work today. Agatha is meeting with the mayor, and it is going to be unpleasant," I moan to Baldwin as we leave the school.

He looks at me all business-like. "You have to. I need you to draw your watchdog away long enough to get some digging done. I'm bringing Ed and Gordon this time."

I wish my feelings were the top consideration, but I understand. "Oh, okay. I'll go then."

AS I SLIP INTO THE LIBRARY, I notice that the front door has been greased. I feel like a silent ghost as I approach Agatha's office where she is talking to the mayor. Her eyes get big and she shakes her head ever so slightly at me. I get the hint. I nod to her over his back and grab my dusting supplies from under the circular desk without making a peep.

Dusting is drudgery today. I really don't want to be here. I'm not sure where I want to be these days, but it's definitely not here. I used to love coming here during the day and reading books all night. I haven't done that since—Dad died. I wonder if I can slip into the basement for a while...Naw. Baldwin isn't down there. He's in our tunnel. I sigh as I get back to work dusting the second-floor books.

A ruckus down below in the atrium catches my attention. Conrad and Mrs. Graight are down there yelling at each other.

"I should be able to pick out a book on my own!"

Mrs. Graight leans on the nearest chair, swaying slightly. "If I leave you alone, you'll talk to her."

Conrad's croaky voice quiets down. "What do you think I'll say? Nothing I say will change anything for me."

"I am under strict orders to keep you away from her...uh, I have to..." Mrs. Graight runs for the lavatory again.

Conrad runs up the stairs as I run toward him. We slip into the lavatory on the second floor. His face is heartbreaking. I put my hands on either side of his sad face. "What can I do to help you?"

His voice fills with venom. "Get me out of here. Let's run away and never come back."

"Where would we go?"

He shrugs. "I don't know, anywhere, how about Grainville?"

I look at my dirty hands and rub them together. "I wish I could, but I can't leave my—"

"Your boyfriend, Baldwin."

My eyebrows come together in confusion. "No, I wasn't going to say that. I was going to say my mom and sister."

"You should get out as soon as you can. My dad is more powerful than ever now that everyone is wearing his GameComs."

"What do they have to do with anything?"

Conrad shakes his head in disgust. "Once you put one on, it's hard to take it off. If my dad posts a deal that's only good at the gaming district, they all come running."

"So, it's not just a gaming machine; it's a communication device?"

He tilts his head back and forth. "Sort of. It's meant to be communication for gaming purposes, but my dad is using it to plant ideas in people's heads."

"What kind of ideas?"

"Ideas that he is innocent. Ideas that they need him. Ideas that you aren't to be trusted."

"I see that you aren't wearing yours. Have you picked a side?"

He shakes his bare wrist like it's freeing. "Yes, I have. Unfortunately, my dad is insisting that I wear it all the time. My babysitter will make sure I put it back on before I go home today."

Knock, knock. "Conrad, I know you're in there. It's time to come out," Mrs. Graight says.

Conrad's mouth tightens, and he closes his eyes. "I know your boyfriend hates me, but I did tell the truth. Don't forget your promise. I don't know how much more of this I can take." He runs his fingers down the side of my face.

Mrs. Graight's voice sounds hysterical. "Conrad, get out here now, or I'm coming in."

He slips out the door before I can respond.

I stare at myself in the mirror for a full ten minutes, hoping to protect Conrad from Mrs. Graight. I don't like what I see. My blonde hair looks stringy and dirty. My skin looks dull, and my eyes look frazzled. What am I doing to myself? I splash some water on my face and dry it off. I'm relieved to see that some of the brown freckles on my face were just dust and dirt that have disappeared. I look at my eyes again. There is more there; what is it? I think it's determination. I want to find justice in this justice-less world for my dad, for Vern, and for Conrad.

As I walk out of the lavatory, Agatha is trudging up the stairs to meet me. She looks sad. "I have bad news, my friend.

The mayor is cutting our budget by another 20%. We will have to shut down two hours earlier each night, we're closing two more rooms before it snows, and Zelma and I will each take a pay cut. I can't afford to pay your wages anymore."

I'm amazed at how sad I am after my whiny attitude about working here today. "Okay, Agatha. I understand."

"I'm glad you dusted the attic and the basement; the mayor wants me to gather up anything that will fetch a price and sell it."

"Are you going to sell the books in the boarded-up rooms?"

"No, I've tried that. The people with money don't want them, and the people who want them don't have money."

I freeze in my shoes. "I'm so sorry, Agatha. Maybe I should keep coming to help you bring things up the basement stairs. I don't want you to hurt your back. You don't have to pay me."

She hands me a few coins and leans toward me. "I wish I could, but the mayor insists that you leave the premises right now and never come back."

"Oh."

It feels like a walk of shame as I leave the library under the mayor's stern gaze. I can't believe he's scowling at me after I've single-handedly made the library look so good.

AS I WALK HOME, I see Baldwin, Ed, and Gordon

walking toward me. I also see a patrolman walking behind them. I stop as they approach me, but Baldwin shakes his head slightly and keeps on walking. I wipe the frustration off my face as Patrolman Darius slinks toward me. "How was work at the library today, Dandra?" he asks.

"It was terrible; I was fired."

He doesn't look surprised. "Really?"

"Yes."

"I'm sorry to hear that. By the way, do you know those guys who just walked by?"

"Yeah. They go to school with me."

He smirks at me. "For some reason, they've been seen loitering around your house more than once."

I have to think fast. "They might have stopped by to get help on homework. There aren't too many of us left at school these days."

Darius raises his eyebrows. "Yeah, that explains why they walked by you like they didn't know who you are just now."

I give him a look that should make him feel stupid. "Uh, I don't know what you're talking about. I need to get home. Have a nice night."

"Don't let me keep you. Good night."

Chapter 56

I AM FUMING AS I STOMP MY WAY into the house. Everley looks up from her book at the table. "It's nice to see you, too."

I feel bad. She always sees me when I'm tired and angry these days. "Do you want to play a game with me?"

"Sure. Which one?"

We walk to the shelf of books and games next to the mantle. The clock says 7:40. Everley starts pulling out my dad's favorite game that takes forever to play. I stop her short. "How about one that takes less than an hour to play?"

Everley scowls at me. "You are no fun anymore! We used

play this with Dad and Conrad all the time. Ever since you banned him from our lives and made Baldwin your boyfriend, my life has been terrible!"

I reach out to her, but she pushes me away. "Everley, I'm sorry."

"I don't want to hear it! I just want you to dump Baldwin—who is the worst boyfriend ever—and take Conrad back." She glares at me and stomps up the stairs.

I guess we won't be playing a game tonight.

THE TUNNEL is definitely emptying out. I'm impressed at the six feet of new space that wasn't there this morning. Baldwin even made some wooden braces up to the ceiling. They don't look as sturdy as my dad's do; we better hurry up and get through to the other side before the whole thing collapses. The guys weren't covered in dirt when I saw them tonight. I wonder what they brushed themselves off with. I see a small broom on the ground. When I pick it up, I'm thrilled to see a note tied to the handle.

D,

I'm pretty sure you-know-who saw us come into your yard tonight. I wouldn't be surprised to see him out there again when we leave. I don't like it. I might try jumping fences from your neighbors' yards if I see him again. I'm determined to keep to my schedule. We'll be out of here December 26th. Ed says that Patrolman Darius has forbidden Patrolman Mark to work on your dad's case anymore. Philip and several other kids our age keep asking us funny questions, too. I think Zane has more people spying on us than we know. Things are getting bad. I don't think your dad is going to get the justice he deserves, and I don't know who all the spies are. Please watch what you say. See you tomorrow.

B

I knew it. Mom comes in to dig as I shove the note into my pocket. "Wow, these boys of yours aren't messing around, are they?"

"Nope."

"I've been thinking about what you said yesterday, and I've decided that this is probably our best plan. Mark just called. He has been ordered off the case. He talked to Darius's boss before he was reassigned, but I don't know if it will do any good. I think I'd rather leave in a month than live under a microscope for the rest of my life."

I look at my mom's pained eyes. "You know that Mark won't come with us, right?"

Mom's eyes drop to the wheelbarrow she's filling with dirt. "Yeah. I know."

I don't want to vocalize it, but I feel the same way about leaving Conrad behind. I wonder if there is any way I can get him away from his father and Mrs. Graight and take him with us. I promised him that I'd be there for him, and I can only be there for him if I take him with me.

Chapter 57

IT STARTS TO SNOW. The weather is horrible. School is horrible. Work would be horrible, but it's over. Ugh.

At school, I tell Baldwin the bad news that I've been fired, and that the library will be closing earlier. I don't get the chance to tell him that Agatha has to sell everything in the basement, though. I'm too concerned about paying off my grandma before we leave when I don't have a job. He suggests that I earn a few coins by shoveling sidewalks. It's a good idea. I don't want to get a new job that will be sad to see me go in a month.

The snow is so deep when I get to Main Street after school, I end up shoveling the library's sidewalks for free because I don't want my old ladies to fall. Agatha peeks her head out the door once I'm done and throws me two coins.

I barely catch them in my huge gloves. I shake my head. "No, I can't take this."

She brings a finger to her lips. "Shh," she says and closes the door. I'm going to miss her.

I convince the clothing store and the candy store to let me shovel their sidewalks for a few coins. I almost ask the hardware store, but I see Jed shoveling their sidewalks himself. He smiles at me and waves as I walk past. After I shovel out the steakhouse, I walk to the autobody shop where Baldwin is shoveling snow to tell him something he isn't going to like.

He looks scruffy yet handsome in his brown winter coat and gloves. "Hey, beautiful."

"Hey."

"Give me five more minutes and I'll be done here." I watch as Baldwin shoves the rest of the snow off the walking path with his shovel like it's nothing.

He smiles at me as he walks into the office. I hear coins dropping into his pocket as he leaves the building. "You really shouldn't have come here." He looks both ways down the street. "But I don't see anyone watching us, so I guess we're okay."

"Did anyone work on the tunnel today?" I ask quietly.

"Yeah, Ed and Marcella did."

"Okay. I hope they weren't caught."

He nods. "Yeah, me too."

I lick my lips as I try to think about what to do. "I'm sorry to have to tell you this, but Agatha has been ordered to sell everything that will fetch a price in the basement."

Baldwin closes his eyes. "Oh, no."

"Yeah."

"Do you know when?"

"No, but I'm guessing soon."

My boyfriend looks around, as if hoping to find an answer. "Great. That means we have to either hide everything we want to keep behind the flag or find somewhere else to live."

I try to sound optimistic. "If you know Darius isn't watching, you can store a few things in the shed or tunnel."

"Thank you. It's going to be tricky getting all of our stuff and eventually all of our bodies into your backyard and through the tunnel without Darius noticing."

I steal a glance at his face as I make the bad news worse. "About that. I want to invite another person to come with us."

He narrows his eyes at me. "Who?"

"Conrad."

He shakes his head. "I was afraid you'd say that. I don't think we can. He's being watched even closer than we are."

I frown. "I know, but he told the truth and now his life is miserable. I want to make it up to him."

Baldwin's eyes grow hard. "Even if we could pull him away from his shadow, he would make our lives miserable. He's a rich, spoiled brat."

"That isn't fair." I shake my head. "He isn't as bad as you think."

"He'll try to take you away from me. I vote 'no' on this."

I stop and stand my ground. "It's my tunnel, and I vote yes."

He shakes his head. "Good luck figuring out how to get him. I have too much on my mind getting the tunnel finished, hiding all our stuff from Agatha, and getting my roommates in warm clothes for the winter to help you. Sorry." His arm goes rigid.

The breath leaves my body. I expected this, but I hate how hollow I feel. We're back to the library again. We walk silently back to the window they use as a door. I was kind enough to shovel a path from the sidewalk to the window and around to the back door, so their footprints in the snow won't give them away. "Bye, Baldwin."

He grabs my hand and pulls me closer. "Don't leave mad. I'm trying to do the most good for the most people here. You've got to see that." He leans forward and gives me a kiss.

I sigh, "I know. I'm just trying to create justice in a corrupt world."

Chapter 58

I DON'T CARE WHAT BALDWIN SAYS. I'm not going to leave Conrad here. As I chip away dirt in the tunnel, I wrack my brain trying to figure out how I can get him away from his father.

Mom wipes the sweat from her face and looks at me. "Since we're leaving the day after Christmas, is it okay if we just get survival supplies for gifts?"

"Yes, that's fine. Do we have money for gifts?"

Mom frowns. "Well, not really. It is going to take every penny to pay off Grandma before we leave. I feel bad leaving her here, but she's too old to leave her retirement village; I really don't want her suffering for food when we're gone, though."

I think about the small amount of coins I earned shoveling snow. "Don't worry about gifts then. We'll just leave with what we can carry."

Mom shakes her head at me defiantly. "Actually, Jim contacted me today at work. He asked if we had any dirt for sale. I told him we had at least two pickup loads now, and we'd have more by the end of the month."

My curiosity gets the better of me. "Did you ask him what he uses it for?"

Mom smiles. "Yes, I did. He said he'd show me when we deliver it."

"I want to come then. I've wondered for years what he does with our dirt."

She nods. "Okay. You can come. We'll deliver it after work."

I imagine what it will take to pull this off. "Wait, won't Darius wonder where the dirt came from?"

"Good point. I'll see if Mark can distract him tomorrow before we leave."

I scratch my arm nervously. "Will that make Darius suspicious?"

"I don't think so. Darius knows that Mark is mad at him. He shouldn't be surprised if he wants to talk about it."

I give in. "Okay. I'll just shovel a few sidewalks after school, and we'll bring Everley too. It'll be a fun family drive in the truck."

Chapter 59

BALDWIN ISN'T AT SCHOOL. That is weird. I sit down in math class next to Adamar and ask, "Where is he?"

He doesn't meet my gaze. "He was escorted into the office as soon as we got to school," he says out of the corner of his mouth.

"Why?"

Adamar's eyes shift nervously. "I don't know. I hope it's nothing, but it could be so many things."

As Mr. Jin walks in, I lower my voice. "Who took him to the office?"

"Patrolman Darius."

My heart sinks. "Oh, no."

"Yeah."

Conrad comes in late with Mrs. Graight. He looks around the room before sitting in front of me. Mrs. Graight huffs her disapproval and sits next to him. Mr. Jin starts into our assignment for the day, not noticing how on edge we all are. He isn't the only one not noticing us. Mrs. Graight's eyes droop and she slides sideways in the desk. When a soft snore comes from her still form, Conrad turns his head and says, "She was fighting with my parents late last night."

Adamar grins and nods his head. "Maybe we'll get a day without spies today."

Conrad smiles. "I hope so."

I lean close to Conrad's ear. "I need to talk to you. Is there any way you can get away from her?"

"The only time I have away from her is when I'm in the lavatory."

"Ew."

The tiniest of smiles curl his lips. "I know, but that's all the time I have to myself anymore."

I wrinkle my nose, imagining what I need to do. "Well, I guess I can make that work. I'll leave class early to go to the lavatory. You meet me in the nearest men's lavatory across the hall. I'll be in the furthest stall."

"Okay."

When I have my assignment done and there are five

minutes left of class, I take my backpack and get permission to use the lavatory. I cringe as I slip inside this room meant for males only. It smells worse than death in here. I fight my gag reflex and slip into the end stall before the person in the middle stall comes out and sees me. It feels like forever before I hear the toilet flush and hear the heavy-set man shuffle to the sink to wash his hands. I hope he washes them twice. As the water stops running, I hear the lavatory door open.

"Hey, Mr. Moreland. How is the science lab these days?" a familiar voice says.

"Ooph, it's fine, but I'm not feeling the best today. You might want to avoid the middle stall."

"Oh, yeah. I will."

"See you around, kid. Enjoy your free moment from house arrest."

"I always try," Conrad says cheerfully. I unlock my stall quietly.

When the lavatory door clangs shut, Conrad opens the door to my stall with a smirk. "That must have been awful."

I shudder. "Yes. It was."

His eyes look at me optimistically. "I hope what you have to say made it worth it to you."

I've missed him. "It is. So, Baldwin and his friends have been helping me finish my dad's tunnel."

The optimism in his eyes is replaced with dismay. "What? Do you need more trouble than you already have?"

I sigh in exasperation. "Trouble is what is driving me to finish it and get out."

"If you want me to help, uh—I can't. I can barely even pee by myself." He looks longingly at me. "Plus, your boyfriend wouldn't enjoy my company in that enclosed space."

I roll my eyes. "I know he wouldn't. In fact, he said he wouldn't help me get you out, but I made you a promise, and I intend to keep it. I want to take you with us when we leave."

Conrad looks at me with his big brown eyes full of uncertainty and regret. "I wish I had been sick that day. I wish I'd kept my big mouth shut and my dad had to deal with the consequences by himself." He takes my hand. "I don't know how to do this, but I want to leave with you. There's nothing to stay for here."

Relief washes over me to hear him say that. "Will you figure out a plan to get away? We're leaving the day after Christmas. I'll come for you, meet you somewhere, or whatever it takes."

I can see the wheels turning in his head. "It's going to be almost impossible. Are you sure I'm worth the trouble?"

"Yes. You are worth the trouble."

Conrad looks more like himself than he has in a long time. He squeezes my hand. "Thank you."

The door to the lavatory bangs open as a couple of guys come in, laughing their heads off. "Hey, Conrad. Your babysitter is asking for you out there."

Conrad's eyes look longingly at me as he shuts the stall door in my face. "I'm sure she is. Tell her I'll be right out."

"Uh, no. I'm not your delivery boy. Go tell her yourself." I hear more laughing with some beeping and buzzing coming from GameComs.

"Fine. I will. Have a nice day, and don't get those things wet."

I hear the door slam. I try not to breathe as the gamers take their merry time laughing and playing their GameComs. The bell finally rings, and the gamers leave. Great, I'm going to be late. I slip out of my stall and down the hall to history.

I slide into the closest seat to the door in history class. I see Conrad give me half a smile across the room. Unfortunately, his is the only smile I see. Baldwin isn't back yet.

Chapter 60

WHEN BALDWIN ISN'T BACK by the end of class, I start worrying that he isn't in the building at all. What if they took him to the detainment center? What if all our hard work has come crashing down around our heels? They could be destroying the tunnel as we speak.

My armpits are soaked through by the time the bell rings. Adamar puts his arm around me and guides me to English class. "You've got to calm down, Dandra. What if they are just keeping him in a room for no reason and watching our reaction? Show them they can't touch you."

His advice makes more sense than I want it to. I force myself to calm down and act normal.

I breathe a sigh of relief when Baldwin comes in as the bell is ringing. I give him a worried look but get nothing back. What does that mean?

At lunch, he takes us outside in the snow to sit at one of the few outdoor tables around the front door. "Dandra, they have a recording device in your house. You have to find it and stop talking around it."

"How do you know?"

"Patrolman Darius just spent the last few hours trying to get me to admit that I am using you for my own purposes, and that I'm trying to take the Chestertons down."

"How did that conversation lead to what's being said in my house? I'm purposely not mentioning you there right now."

My last statement makes Baldwin wince. "It didn't. I just heard Darius whisper to his fellow patrolman that he heard your sister tell you that I am the worst boyfriend ever and she wants you to take Conrad back."

The ugly truth sets in. She did say that in our house. In our living room to be exact. How did a recording device get into our living room?

When was the last time we had a patrolman in our house? I suddenly remember Patrolman Darius coming to our house and poking around without anything really important to say that first time. I bet that's when he planted it.

Charlisa snuggles into Adamar as she shivers. "Why are we talking out here? I'm freezing."

Baldwin lowers his voice. "I'm pretty sure they have recording devices everywhere we go in this school."

Gordon waves him off. "Our classrooms are easy enough to plant things in, but not even the teachers know where we will eat lunch each day."

Baldwin nods. "Yeah, that makes me think someone else, who pays regular attention to us, is telling him."

I have no idea who is left to do that. "Who? Philip and Zane's other gaming fans only started spying on us once they dropped out of school."

Baldwin doesn't meet my eyes. "I don't think it's those guys."

"Who, then?"

"Conrad."

Chapter 61

I DON'T KNOW WHAT TO THINK. Is Conrad still spying on me for his dad? I guess it has been a usual conversation for them all these years, but his dad has ruined his life. Surely the sad Conrad I see each day isn't faking it.

Oh, no. I told him about our plans. What do I do now?

There hasn't been any new snow, so nobody wants me to shovel them out today. I decide to stop by the library as a patron for once. Agatha is pleased to see me. "I miss you so much, Dandra! That mayor is the worst this city has ever had. I can't believe he cut our budget back twice as much as he usually does when the library is looking so good and more people are using it."

I nod sympathetically with her. "We knew my time here was coming to an end, though."

"I am so mad that he is making me sell everything in the basement to cover the cost of the weekend janitor. My back is going to break."

"When are you starting all of that?"

"Tomorrow. He's coming to check on my progress the day after that," she says as she rolls her eyes.

Oh, no. I need to warn my friends. "Uh—I could help you, Agatha."

She shakes her head sadly. "No, I can't let you. He made me promise. It's almost like he has a personal problem with you or something."

I can imagine that his personal problem has a lot to do with Zane Chesterton's monthly donation to his coin purse. I smile sadly. "Oh, well. I'll just pop upstairs and get a detective novel if that's all right."

"Help yourself, sweetheart."

As soon as I enter the mystery and detective book room, I rip a sheet of paper out of my notebook and write a note to Baldwin telling him that Agatha is coming down to take things tomorrow. I sign it "D" and address the outside of the note to "B."

As I kneel on the floor of the mystery and detective novel

room looking for the secret hole to the basement, Charlisa surprises me by joining me. "Hey, Dandra. How are you handling all the things Baldwin said about Conrad?"

I shake my head. "Not good. I don't know what to do."

Charlisa notices me looking around the bookshelf. "I can help you find what you're looking for." She points to a note sticking out of her pocket. She looks at me like I'm the most pathetic person she's ever seen. "You know, you're not friends with Conrad anymore, so just stop talking to him and avoid talking anywhere around him."

My eyebrows reach together in frustration. "Have you failed to notice what happened when he told on his dad?"

Charlisa shrugs. "Yeah, but he's getting what he deserves, don't you think?"

I frown. "Nobody deserves to be punished for telling the truth."

She gives me a sympathetic smile as she stacks all the Steadman mysteries on the window sill. She pulls a false back off the shelf, takes the intricately folded note out of her coat pocket, and drops it into the hole she has just exposed.

I drop my note down the hole too. As we put the shelf back together, she turns and looks at me. "I know you're struggling with this plan of Baldwin's, and believe me, you're not the only one."

I look at her sideways. "Are you going to leave with us?"

She nods. "I'm going to sneak out in the night if I can, but my mom is the lightest sleeper in the world. It's not likely to work."

"Can you convince her and your dad to come with us?"

Charlisa snorts. "No. She is a control freak. If we leave with you, she won't be able to handle not being in charge."

I imagine how she must feel. I'm lucky that everyone I care about is coming with me. "I'm so sorry."

"I know. Just try to get the border opened up once you're on the other side, okay?" She shrugs. "Mom can't control me forever."

As if to prove how wrong she is, her mom walks in and says, "It's time to go, Charlisa. What book did you choose?"

Charlisa grabs the first Steadman off the shelf. "This one. See you at school, Dandra."

I smile sadly. "Okay. Bye." I give my book selection the same amount of thought as Charlisa does. It's a lonely walk down the stairs to the check-out desk.

Agatha pauses before giving me my detective novel back. "Goodbye, Dandra."

It's almost like she knows I'm leaving this country for good. "Goodbye, Agatha."

Chapter 62

I AM CONSCIOUSLY AWARE of all the people with GameComs on their arms as I walk home. They all seem to be gravitating to the gaming district like ants gravitating to a jelly doughnut on the ground. I wonder if Zane sent them a message about half-off games today or something. I overhear the gamer in front of me talking to his friend.

"...free points and free candy shakes. The last time I got a message from the gaming district, I had just told my brother that I wasn't going to the gaming district ever again. I would just play on my GameCom at home until my points were gone."

"So?"

"Less than a minute later, I get a message from the gaming district saying that every customer at the gaming district that day would get 500 free points and a megajuice beverage of their choice."

"Okay…"

"It's almost like someone from the gaming district was listening to me say that I wouldn't go there anymore, so they offered me free stuff so I'd would."

His friend shakes his head dismissively. "No way. It was just a coincidence."

"Ha ha. Yeah, you're probably right." They keep marching like ants to their prize.

My brain starts racing a million miles a minute. What if this guy's story isn't a coincidence? I hope there is someone in the tunnel to talk to right now. I walk faster to get home. I don't see anyone following me, so that's a relief. As I turn the last corner, I see Patrolman Mark drag Patrolman Darius down the street with him.

Oh, yeah. We're taking dirt to Jim tonight. I rush to the shed and down the ladder as fast as I can. Baldwin, Gordon, and Adamar are at the end of the tunnel digging away. My words come faster than my brain can decipher them. "The GameComs are the spies, not Conrad. They may know everything about everything!"

Baldwin sets his shovel down and squeezes my shoulders. "Say that again—slower this time."

"I overheard some gamers saying that they get messages from the gaming district that relate to what they say out loud. I think that the GameComs are microphones to Zane." I finally catch my breath. "I don't think Conrad is spying on us, but his GameCom might be."

Baldwin tilts his head to the side as he thinks about what I just said. "Yeah. That makes so much sense. We have to avoid those things like the plague." I nod in agreement. He looks at me. "Do you think you can convince Conrad to take his off?"

"I can try tomorrow, but he told me that his dad is making him wear it."

Baldwin's face shows no sympathy. "That is almost as unfortunate as all of us getting kicked out of our home tomorrow," he says sarcastically.

I reach out and squeeze his arm. "What are you going to do?"

"Ed and Marcella are packing up everything that is important and storing it behind the flag right now. The problem is, we won't fit in there, too."

"Agatha might sell the flag and then she'll see your hidden room."

"I've made a lock for the door that only I can unlock. Agatha isn't that ambitious. Our stuff should be fine."

"Where are you going to sleep?"

"We'll stay there tonight, but tomorrow, I don't know."

"We could always see if Vern's house is open," Adamar says.

"Poor Vern," I mutter.

Baldwin squeezes my shoulder. "We're ahead of schedule. I may just stay...in here until it's finished."

I am filled with doubt about that. "Hmm. I don't think my mom will like that, and it's freezing down here." Baldwin doesn't look deterred. I sigh. "I'm leaving to sell dirt to someone right now; let me think about it."

He kisses my forehead. "Okay. Drive safe."

Chapter 63

I HAVE SO MUCH ON MY MIND, I'm yet again a terrible sister to Everley. She elbows me hard in the side. "You are crossing the line into my space; move over."

"This isn't a big truck, sis. Sorry."

Mom clears her throat. "We are lucky to be out in this truck at all. Mark took Darius away just in time." I see a smile light her lips as she says Mark's name.

I hope I'm imagining things. "Have you kissed him, Mom?"

"Mark?" she asks.

"Obviously."

She bites her lip for a second. "I'll tell you if—you tell me. Have you kissed Baldwin?"

"Uh—yes, I've kissed him."

Mom's eyes bulge. "Huh. I have not kissed Mark."

Everley rolls her eyes and elbows me again. "Did you kiss Conrad?"

I look at her fiery eyes, and I can't lie to her. "He kissed me once."

Everley asks me point blank, "Which one did you like better?"

Mom raises her voice. "Okay, that's enough kiss talk for today. Besides, we're here."

Jim's house is enormous. His house, his garage, his shop, and his fence are all tall enough for giants to live in. I can't believe that this is the guy who buys our dirt.

I jump out of the truck, thankful to be away from Everley's elbows. A tall man with a curly blonde beard comes out of his house to greet us. "Hello, Metty family. I'll open the shop door and you can just pull in and I'll unload the dirt."

Mom obeys his instructions while I stand there watching. He wasn't kidding. He and his husky-looking wife start shoveling the dirt into a pile on a tarp in his shop. My curiosity gets the better of me. "What are you going to do with this dirt?"

He pauses long enough to point to the back of his shop. "Can you see my kiln? I make it into bricks."

"Do you sell the bricks?"

He chuckles. "No. Not these bricks. Come on back. I'll show you what I'm making in the backyard."

I follow Jim through a door into his backyard. My jaw drops. I didn't realize that this house is next to the border wall, like ours, except that the fence that keeps us out of no man's alley is much taller here. It's almost as tall as the border wall. There is a huge staircase made of bricks taking up most of the backyard, and it is approaching the top half of the government-mandated fence.

My breath catches in my throat. "I can't believe it. I thought my dad was the only one crazy enough to do something like this."

"Sorry to disappoint you. Your dad and I used to be in an invention club together years ago. I figured out pretty quickly that your dad was digging under the border wall. Since I'm a mason, I have multiple kilns. I brought this older one back here once I bought a newer, bigger one for my business. I thought to myself, I can get to the other side, too, if I go over the wall. I don't want to be found out, so I've designed my whole property to hide it."

"Why is the government fence so much taller here than at our house?"

"This is where Layland started its fence to keep us away from the border wall, but it soon realized that it took too long and was too expensive to keep building it this tall all the way around. It just goes to show that we've been a lazy country from the beginning."

Jim's words amaze me. "I didn't realize that." I look at the big man in front of me curiously. "Why bother with all this? Why do you want to leave?"

Jim snorts. "I hate it here. I can't find good workers anymore, there's always plastic trash blowing into my kilns and ruining my bricks, but most importantly, my ancestors came from the United Cities." He looks towards the shop for a second. "My wife and I can't have children, and since my brother died, we have no family here anymore." He pats the huge base of his giant staircase. "My great-grandfather was a twin who grew up in a big family in the United Cities. He had an ugly falling out with his family when he was a teenager and paid a smuggler to get him out of the country. The border wall wasn't quite finished back then. I've always wondered how much family I have on that side of the wall," he says as he nods to it.

"What was your great-grandfather's name?"

"Herbert Yesterly."

"Did he ever regret his decision and try to go back?"

"Once they finished the wall, there was no way back. When he was on his deathbed, he kept saying that he wished he could see his twin brother before he died, but obviously that couldn't happen." Jim rubs both eyes with one hand for a second. "I think about that all the time. That's the real reason I started this staircase. I want to do what great-grandpa wished he could do—reconnect with our family."

I nod. "I get it. I'm just trying to figure out how you'll get across the fifteen feet of no man's land to the United Cities."

He walks me to the side of his huge backyard and pulls up the longest tarp I've ever seen. Underneath it are four gigantic cross beams at least 25 feet in length. "We'll make the fences on each side of no man's alley into a bridge with these."

That sounds like a long, scary walk to me. "How will you get down the other side?"

He walks me back into his shop where he pulls out some rope, grappling hooks, and harnesses. "We'll lower ourselves down."

I hope the doubt in my eyes isn't obvious. "Wow, I hope you've been practicing; that sounds hard."

Jim nods. "We have. My wife is the toughest woman I know."

I look behind me at his wife, who is shoveling dirt onto the tarp faster than any man I know. Jim hands my mom a sack of coins and looks at us both seriously. "Are you leaving sooner than I am?"

Mom whispers, "Yes, much sooner—within the month."

"If you end up leaving anyone behind, and if they are someone you can trust, send them to me. I'll be done with the staircase in about a year. I'll need extra hands on my side to get the cross beams placed correctly."

Those words are music to my ears. "I know of at least one person who probably won't make it out with us. I'll give her your name and address. I may also have a two-way radio to give you, so we can keep in touch from the other side."

"Thank you. Now go get that next pickup load of dirt for me."

Chapter 64

MOM AND EVERLEY ARE QUIET as we go home. I think we all know that our day of departure is approaching fast, and there are many people we will be leaving behind.

There is no patrolman anywhere to be seen as we back the pickup into the bushes, and there is a wheelbarrow of dirt waiting for us behind the bushy barrier. I'm glad; that means Baldwin is probably still here.

Mom runs into the house to get an update from Mark on where he and Darius are. Everley and I try to climb down into the tunnel, but Baldwin, Adamar, and Gordon are lifting a wheelbarrow up to the surface. We help them get it up as best we can. Baldwin is positively beaming as he comes up the ladder. "I can hear something at the end of the tunnel. I'm almost positive we're into the United Cities!"

"What can you hear?"

"I can't tell for sure, but I'm guessing it's muffled voices."

A new fear overtakes me. "What if we come out in the worst place ever? Like a patrolman center, or a school yard?"

Baldwin's excitement won't be extinguished. "There's no turning back now, Dandra. We'll figure it out. But first, we need to get all this loose dirt out of here and into your truck."

I'm so glad these three boys are here. It would take Mom, Everley, and me forever to move the dirt and fill the truck. They make it look easy.

Once the truck is full, we see that there is at least another truck-full left. Mom tells us, "Mark says that he convinced Darius's superior to go over all of Mark's findings about Zane Chesterton tonight—with Darius. Mark is waiting outside the office for them right now. They are going to be in the office for at least a couple of hours." She climbs into the truck and starts it up. "Have the next load ready for me when I get back."

I nod. "Okay, Mom."

Baldwin waves. "No problem, Mrs. Metty."

I don't think Baldwin wants to sleep on the floor in the library basement tonight, because he hauls dirt out of the tunnel like a madman even after the rest of us tire and eventually stop. I can't handle hearing the boys' stomachs growling anymore, so Everley and I go inside to make some kind of dinner for everyone. We don't have any meat or cheese, but we have quite a few potatoes and onions, so we make some quick fried potatoes for everyone.

I think even Everley's cold heart softens while watching the boys' wide eyes as they enter our house and devour every last bite of mediocre fried potatoes. Gordon winks at Everley as he finishes his seconds and says, "If this little lady will cook this kind of food every day, maybe I will move into the tunnel with Baldwin for a few days."

I can see her fighting to hide a smile as she gathers up the dirty dishes. Baldwin rolls his eyes at Gordon and gives my hand a squeeze. Adamar looks like he's going to fall asleep at the table until we hear the truck pull in.

Baldwin is instantly on his feet. "Get up! Let's get that dirt out of here."

Adamar groans and Gordon gives Everley one last wink before leaving with Baldwin out the door.

Mom says that there still aren't any patrolman out there, so she, Everley, and I start shoveling the dirt pile from behind the bushes into the truck. I never thought I'd see the day when we would use all three of these new shovels at once, but here we are. We can hear the boys grunting and groaning as they haul both wheelbarrows up and down the ladder hole.

It only takes us an hour to fill the pickup for a third time tonight. Mom looks tired, so I insist that she take Everley to help keep her awake as she drives. Adamar and Gordon leave to help finish hiding their stuff and get some shut eye.

I want to collapse into Baldwin's arms and just do nothing, but he has other ideas.

"I know you're tired, but aren't you dying to have a peek into the United Cities?" he asks excitedly.

"How do you know if we're under their wall yet?"

"I'm sure we are. We're way ahead of schedule. Here, I'll prove it to you. He pulls a notebook out of his backpack and starts drawing calculations on a piece of paper and talking so fast that I can't keep up.

I rub my tired eyes. "Okay, okay. I believe you. Digging straight up is going to be a nightmare for our eyeballs, and it will take forever. There's five feet of dirt up here," I say as I pat the ceiling.

Baldwin shakes his head. "Not with this." He pulls a weird corkscrew-looking thing out from behind the stack of shovels. "This is an auger. I've read about them, and I found this one at the dump a few years ago."

He looks at me expecting praise or something. I give him half a smile. "That's great?"

"Here. I need you, and maybe the ladder to help me keep it steady. I will turn the crank."

I don't want to burst his bubble, so I agree even though it means I will be eating dirt. It takes a minute to find the right spot for the ladder to do most of the supporting. Baldwin insists that we angle it sideways away from us. I put my dad's old work gloves on so I don't get burned from the friction. "You know this is only going to make a hole skinny enough for a fence post, right?" I ask with a yawn.

"I know, I just want to see the other side, not go through tonight." Baldwin starts cranking the handle like his life depends on it. I make him stop for a minute so I can find my dad's old wide-brimmed hat to protect my head and face from the spray of dirt. I doze off a couple of times standing there, much to his dismay. What does he expect? This has been a long day. His excited voice startles me awake after an hour. "Wake up! I think I just broke through. Hand me the flashlight."

I wipe the dirt and sleep from my eyes and look up. I don't see anything but a narrow hole. There is a definite sound coming through. It sounds like singing. When Baldwin shines a flashlight into the hole, sure enough, the light disappears. I start laughing and crying at the same time. He wraps me in his arms and laughs with me. I can't believe it! The United Cities is just right there. I am breathing their air right now. Baldwin picks me up and twirls me around.

He grins like he's never grinned before. "We did it! We can get out of here within the next few days. It won't matter if we get kicked out of the library, or if everyone's GameComs are spying on us. We're free!"

I'm so tired and happy, I just melt into his arms and let him hold me. His lips find mine right as I realize how late it is.

I think I disappoint him when I lean back and say, "Let's go tell my mom. She should be back by now. Then I'll make you a bed up there in the shed."

"Okay," he says as he kisses me again.

A thought comes to me. "Will you give your radio to Jim? His staircase over the wall will be ready in about a year. I think we should stay in touch with people on this side once we're out."

Baldwin frowns slightly. "I want to use it—to stay in touch, though."

"Won't Ernestine let you use her radio?"

Baldwin's face lights up. "Yeah, I'm sure she will. Smart thinking. I should give Jim my radio."

I'm happier than I've been in days as we climb up the ladder. The smile on my face doesn't last once I'm above ground. My mom is looking at me in anguish from the doorway of the shed as Patrolman Darius steps out from behind her.

Chapter 65

"I KNEW THERE WAS SOMETHING FISHY going on back here," Darius says with a leer.

Mom's shaking voice speaks up. "There is no law against digging a hole on your own property."

"But there is a law about tampering with government-owned fences and leaving the country." He clicks his tongue and shakes his head. "I wondered why I kept finding you around here, Baldwin Kole. I can't believe I listened to your lies for hours on end at the school. I should have hauled you off to the detainment center then like Zane Chesterton wanted me to."

Baldwin's eyes look unnaturally calm, and then he bolts out

the door, pushing Darius down as he goes. We all stand there in shock for a second, but then Darius jumps to his feet and takes off after him. Our poor privacy bushes will never be the same. I just hope my boyfriend has enough energy left to sprint.

MOM HOLDS ME ON THE COUCH AS I CRY into her shoulder. What is Darius going to do to him? What is he going to do to us? When the phone rings, Mom gets up and shakily answers it. "H-hello?" She immediately breathes a sigh of relief. "I'm so glad. I know. I understand. Thank you for everything. I don't know what I would do without you, Mark. Bye."

I try to read between the lines of relief and sadness on my mom's face. "What is it?"

"Darius didn't catch Baldwin, but he's on his way to board up our shed—and take us to the detainment center. He's having a concrete truck fill in the tunnel as soon as possible. Mark says that is most likely tomorrow evening."

My heart sinks below my toenails. "Oh." How could I have been so stupid? I have worked so hard to find justice in a justice-less place. I have worked so hard to help my family survive without Dad. I have worked so hard to get the people I care about out of here. What good did it do? I've bruised and broken my body and mind for nothing. We're all going to the detainment center anyway.

The sound of hammers pounding nails into wood close to the house makes me jump.

Mom frowns. "I guess they're here. That was fast."

Knock, knock. Mom trembles as she opens the door. Darius struts into our house like he owns the place. He walks over to Dad's old clock and pulls a small device from underneath it. "I won't be needing this anymore. Say goodbye to your tunnel and to your freedom. The tunnel will be filled in as soon as the local company can do it, and I'm going to have to take you to the detainment center."

Mom starts crying. "That was my husband's project. Why do you have the right to punish us for his actions?"

"It wasn't him I found in there tonight; it was your daughter and a known troublemaker. Go gather a small bag of essentials and decide where you want me to take your youngest daughter."

Mom and I wobble like old ladies as we walk up the stairs. I've never felt so scared for my family. We move as silently as mimes as we pack a change of clothes for each of us and some toiletries. I try to hide my fear as I wake up Everley and bring her downstairs. She is not thrilled. "Why aren't you in bed? It's the middle of the night; I want to sleep." I shush her as I force her onto the couch next to mom and me.

Knock, knock. I stand up to open the door, but Darius beats me to it. Mark and some man I don't know barge in.

The man I don't know looks at the bag my mom is holding and the tears on her cheeks before turning to Darius and demanding, "What is the meaning of this, Darius? You ran out of our meeting early to come here and harass a widow?"

Darius's face fills with righteous indignation. "Patrolchief Miller, I'm taking them to the detainment center for digging a hole under the border wall and trying to escape."

"Have you personally examined the tunnel?"

Darius looks flustered for the first time ever. "Well, no."

"Patrolman Mark here has, and he says it is an underground mushroom garden that this widow's husband made before he died."

Darius looks at Mark and the other man like he hopes they're kidding. "You can't honestly believe that. The hole is clearly aiming for the border wall."

The man nods. "I agree that it is too close to the border wall to be allowed. It will still be filled in tomorrow, but I cannot in good conscience detain this widow and her daughters for something her husband did."

Darius's face turns red. "This is ridiculous. They are not harmless little angels. They have underhandedly tried to blame Zane Chesterton..."

"Hold it right there. Why do you care so much about Zane Chesterton's well-being? This woman's husband was hit in front of his house by a car that looks exactly like his own according to an eye-witness, and the story was confirmed by Chesterton's own son. We should not let Zane Chesterton run our department anymore." Darius looks like he has been kicked in the teeth. Patrolchief Miller exhales before saying, "We should all take a deep breath and ensure that this widow gets justice."

Darius points at my face with all the venom he can muster. "That girl and an anti-gamer were in that tunnel tonight. They were not picking mushrooms."

Patrolchief Miller turns to my mother. "Mrs. Metty, what do you think they were doing in there?"

Mom gulps as she looks at me. "Judging by the flushed color of their cheeks, I would guess that they were kissing."

I make a show of my shock. "Mom! Seriously?"

Patrolchief Miller turns to Darius. "Darius, were they flushed like they had been kissing?"

Darius rolls his eyes. "Yes, they were. But the boy—"

Patrolcheif Miller smiles and cuts him off. "There you go, Darius. I don't think teenagers kissing in a secret place is worth all this fuss." Darius almost interrupts, but the patrolchief stops him. "I will bring them all in tomorrow evening for questioning, but they will not be taken to the detainment center in the middle of the night like criminals. The tunnel will be filled in as you scheduled it, so accept your wins and take your losses gracefully, or you will be put on probation."

If Darius's looks could kill, Mark would be dead. "Fine. I'll see you both in the office tomorrow. Good evening." Darius somehow refrains from slamming the door on the way out.

"I'm sorry for keeping you and your young ones up so late, Mrs. Metty. Please accept my apologies. I'm afraid your mushroom garden will have to be filled in tomorrow at 7:00 pm because of its proximity to the border wall. I will also have to question you about the reason it was created. But that can happen after you get off work tomorrow. Please get some sleep, and I'll see you again tomorrow at my office."

"I understand. Thank you, Patrolchief," Mom says quietly. Her eyes meet Mark's and something sweet passes wordlessly between them before she leads the men out the door.

I can't believe Mark lied for us. He saved us—well, for now. I feel like such a jerk for the way I've always talked about him. "Mom, did you tell Mark about the tunnel?"

Mom's lips tremble as she shakes her head. "Not really. He asked me why I always have dirt under my fingernails last night, and I said that I was trying to finish an underground project that Dad started. He asked if it was some kind of underground mushroom garden, and I told him it was something like that. I'm as surprised as you are about what he said tonight. Actually—I'm not." She puts a hand over her mouth and bolts for her room.

It's 2:00 in the morning, and I should get some sleep. It's going to be a long day tomorrow. I trudge up the stairs to my room and try to sleep, but I can't. I don't know if I'll ever sleep again.

KNOCK, KNOCK. I FROWN as Darius and two other patrolmen push their way past my sister into our kitchen as we're eating breakfast. He smiles at me like he's just won the lottery. "I had a feeling you'd need some—escorts to help you get to school and work today. You have an appointment with my superior tonight for some serious questioning. Until then, I've made it my business to keep you on your regular schedule."

I glare at him. "How kind of you."

"I try."

I wish I knew what to do, but I don't, so I just glare at the three patrolmen. "Which of you guys is escorting me to school?"

Darius raises his hand with a cruel grin. "I will take you to school for your first hour, but then you have a special appointment that I need to get you to at 10:00."

"An appointment with whom?"

"Zane Chesterton."

"Does the patrolchief know about this?"

"What he doesn't know won't hurt him."

Oh, no.

Chapter 66

I FEEL LIKE A CRIMINAL as Darius and his stooge walk Everley and me to our schools. Once Everley and her "escort" enter the low-level school, I turn to Darius and say, "I'd really like to know what is in this for you. My whole world has collapsed too many times to count. Why do I have to endure this too? Just lock me in the detainment center and be done with it."

"You are a confused and over-dramatic teenager. Your parents have led you down a dangerous path, but it's not too late for you." Whatever that means.

If I thought school was awkward before, this is just unreal.

The halls part down the middle as soon as everyone sees me with Darius. I am positively sweating as I enter math class. I hope he's not here.

Baldwin is not in class, thankfully, but Adamar and Ed are. They take one look at Darius and avert their eyes from me for the rest of the class. Conrad isn't afraid to look at me. His eyes are sympathetic. He knows exactly how I feel right now; I just wish I could communicate with him. He glares at Darius and then turns on his GameCom and plays some game that keeps repeating, "Do you wanna fight me?" extremely loudly over and over again. Mr. Jin glares at him and asks, "Can you please turn that game off, Conrad?"

Conrad smiles contemptuously and says, "Nope."

"Can you at least turn it down?"

"Nope."

Mr. Jin and Mrs. Graight look at Darius for some help or authority. He glares at Conrad but doesn't say anything. I don't think he wants to yell at the son of the man who pays him.

I can't focus and not just because of Conrad's "fight me" game. What's the point of doing anything? I am on my way to see Zane Chesterton. He owns this town. Even though he is a criminal, and I'm not, I'm at his mercy.

When the bell rings, Mrs. Graight tries to haul Conrad and his loud game out of the room as fast as she can. I hear her say, "You are being disrespectful. You shouldn't play games on that thing in class."

He growls back, "I don't care what you think. I'm going to play this game all day long." Darius gets up and whispers something into Conrad's ear.

When his back is turned, Adamar slips me a note on his way out the door. I recognize the handwriting the "D" on the outside is written in. It brings a slight smile to my face.

Darius tap my shoulder when I don't get out of my desk. I glare at him. "I don't want to go. Zane Chesterton isn't a patrolman; I shouldn't have to see him if I don't want to."

"He isn't a patrolman, but I am, so get up."

I get up and walk out of the classroom with him. I wonder if my freedom is at an end. I want to read my note just in case. "I need to go to the lavatory."

"I don't believe it."

"I haven't gone yet today. I won't last all the way to the gaming district in the cold winter air."

"Fine. You have three minutes."

I burst into the female lavatory and lock myself in the end stall. The note is out of my pocket in one second flat.

D,

I'm staying at an old friend's house for a while. M, G, and I will be finishing the way out while everyone is at school and work. If there is someone guarding it, G is going to take him out. I hate to do that, but we are out of choices. I am taking my radio to J as soon as I can slip out. E and A will join us after school. I don't know if C can get away today yet, hopefully they can make it work. Get little E and your M packed and out before 7:00 tonight. After that, PD said he would have it full of concrete. I'm so sorry it has come to this. Do whatever it takes, use lethal force if needed. I'll see you where the grass is greener.

B

My hands shake as I tear the note up and flush it down the toilet. I have so little time; I don't know if I can get Mom and Everley through the boarded-up shed and through the skinny hole into the United Cities by 7:00. There are three full-grown men I'll have to dispose of—and then there's Conrad. *Knock, knock.*

"I'm coming," I say as I wash my trembling hands.

Darius opens the door a crack. "Let's go."

Chapter 67

TEARS ROLL DOWN MY CHEEKS as I walk with Darius to the gaming district. My legs make a swishing sound as I walk through the trash blowing around me. The sound makes me feel like I'm swimming in an ocean so deep and with so many victims drowning around me that I'll have to pick and choose who will survive. That is if I survive the gigantic weight tied around my own neck first. I take a deep breath and let it out slowly to calm my pounding heart. To be fair, I thought my own freedom was done for just 30 minutes ago. Now I know that there is a way out, but just until 7:00. I have to get rid of three patrolmen before then. How on earth can I do that?

The Gaming District's bright flashing lights mock me as I approach the last place on earth that I want to be. "Mr. Chesterton wants to help you see the error of your ways, Dandra. Your rebellious path has come to an end. I would take the offered olive branch if I were you."

"I'll think about it."

"Fine. Follow me."

I get to see the inner office of the gaming district. The furnishings are so new and expensive-looking, I'm afraid to touch anything. I see Conrad's mother, Jerika, sitting at a desk next to a big mahogany door that says, "Zane Chesterton, Owner" on it. She looks terrible. I mean, her clothes and hair are beautiful like always, but she has lost a lot of weight, and her eyes look dark and sunken in.

She looks at me, forces a smile, then says, "Zane is expecting you. Go right in."

Darius opens the door for me and ushers me in. I walk into the fanciest room I've ever seen, and take a seat in the most comfortable office chair I've ever sat in. Darius looks at the seat next to me and asks, "Do you want me to stay, Mr. Chesterton?"

Zane takes a GameCom out of a box and sets it on his desk. "No, that's all right. I'd like to talk to Miss Dandra alone for a moment. Just check her for recording devices first."

Darius is rougher than he has to be as he searches me from head to toe. "Okay, she's clean. Just call if you need me."

I feel used and helpless as the door takes an unnaturally

long time to click shut. When it does, Zane Chesterton, my best friend's dad and my dad's killer, gives me a look that could kill.

"Why did you turn my son against me, Dandra?"

I have so little to lose, I don't hold back. "You turned your son against you when you killed my father and asked him to lie about it."

"You realize that your man is off the investigation, right?"

I think of my mom's love-sick boyfriend and how he lied for us last night. My voice chokes as I say, "Yes. Believe it or not, after the worst night of my life last night, I figured out that my man is out, and your man is in. He is very proud to be in charge of the investigation now, and he's been spying on me and escorting me around all day."

He laughs humorlessly at me. "You have lost, Dandra. It's your word against mine, and unfortunately for you, my word holds more weight than yours."

"Only because your coin purse holds more weight than mine."

Zane nods his head. "Yes, that too." He looks at the GameCom on his desk. "Do you have any idea how much one of these costs?"

"No."

"If you still had your crummy little library job, it would take you three years to pay this off."

Is my life an open book? "How do you know I lost my

job?" Now that I think about it, I probably said something into Conrad's GameCom.

Zane shrugs. "Oh, the mayor and I have been collaborating on the best way to shut that place down for years. I doubt the decrepit librarians will last another year at their current pay. Once they leave, we'll shut it down."

"Why do you care if it's open or not?"

"When people have questions, I want them to turn to— more modern sources than the library for answers. Plus, I have reason to believe it is a haven for known lawbreakers."

I sneer in disgust. "You sound so noble."

"Dandra, I want to reinvent myself with you. I am not a bad man. I donate money to many worthy causes, including your father's funeral luncheon, if you'll recall."

I feel anger surge through my veins. "That funeral wouldn't have been needed if you weren't a murderer!"

Zane touches his chest gingerly. "Ow, that is the first time anyone has dared to accuse me directly. It kind of stings."

I wish I could scream, but I stay composed. "Did you do it on purpose?" I gulp as I imagine the answer. "It won't hurt you to tell me. I've lost everything; you've already won."

Zane takes a glass of some fancy drink, swirls the ice around and gulps it down. "Yes. I did it on purpose. I was about to lose my favorite ability on the GameComs because of him. He knew the right thing to say to the right people, and I was so close. I knew that he passed my house on his way home from work every day. When I saw him pedaling down the street on his miserable bicycle, I backed out as fast as I could."

I just sit there in shock. He admitted it. His smile doesn't make me feel any better. A tear rolls down my cheek as I relive the scene of my dad's smashed bicycle and the bloodstain that still lingers on Oak Street. I have to keep it together. I only have until 7:00 to save the rest of my family. I wipe the tear and say, "At least I'll always know that my dad died protecting the ones he loved and standing up for what he knew was right."

"I'm glad that gives you comfort."

His comment makes me realize that the shy Dandra I used to be has disappeared. "Can you tell me one more thing?"

He shrugs and pours himself another drink. "Why not?"

"Does Conrad know you did it on purpose?"

He looks at me for a second before answering. "He didn't know until just recently. He believed it was an accident until he overheard my wife and I—having a late-night discussion."

I grit my teeth. "How can you look at yourself in the mirror every day when you know you've made him look like a lunatic?"

"You almost sound like you care about him."

His statement gives me pause. "I do—he's my friend."

"I still don't understand what he sees in you. You are completely indifferent to him. You are pretty enough, I guess, but our friends have daughters who are absolutely stunning. You have kept us up-to-date on the intellectual discussions brewing in the city, which is nice for me, but I still don't get what Conrad gets out of the deal."

I think of how much Conrad has been there for me through the years before I ask, "How long have you known about our tunnel?"

"What tunnel?"

"The tunnel Darius is having filled in today."

"I don't know what you're talking about, but I'm glad that Darius is on top of whatever it is." Zane leans forward. "I'm not a terrible person, Dandra. I did take your father from you, and I feel bad about that. As a matter of fact..." He points to the GameCom on his desk. "I want you to have this. I want you to see that your dad was fighting for the wrong cause." He hands the ugly metal contraption to me. "It's time to turn a new leaf, you and I. How about this. I'll consult the academic community before designing any more gaming machines, and you can give this gaming device a chance. You could be a model for it. I'm sure seeing it on your arm will send the kind of message that will get Darius off your back...."

I look at the ugly device in my hands. Is he saying that if I wear it, I can trade my flesh-and-blood spy for a mechanical spy?

I only have until 7:00. "I accept your offer," I say as I strap the thing onto my arm. He looks shocked at my willingness.

"That's a good girl. Maybe things will turn out just fine for both of us."

I can't lose time. "Can you teach me how to play the 'fight me, fight me' game?"

He is completely stunned. "I don't have time for that, but I'm sure my assistant can help you."

"Thank you. I never could have afforded this on my own. I'll wear it everywhere I go. Can I walk myself home now without Darius?"

Zane taps his fingers together. "Let's see if you really keep it on and behave yourself for the rest of the day. If you do, I'll make sure Darius doesn't bother you tomorrow."

My heart sinks, but I can still make my plan work if I'm very lucky. "Okay."

Zane looks at me curiously as he yells, "Darius! We're done here." Darius opens the door. "Please help my assistant teach Dandra how to use the GameCom and then escort her back to school."

"Yes, sir."

I approach the pimply, young assistant sitting next to Conrad's mom. "Can you teach me how to play the 'fight me' game?"

He pushes his glasses up his nose. "Uh, sure. I think you mean the Title Fight for Dominance. It is a game that requires you to compete with other gamers through the GameCom Community. Come closer. I can show you how to do it, but first you have to create a gamer name."

I wrinkle my nose in annoyance. "Can't I just be Dandra?"

"No, most people want to create a new persona with their gamer name." When that doesn't excite me, he shrugs. "You at least need to add a number."

I think about what will tell the gamer I'm trying to reach who I am. "Okay, I'll be LibraryDuster1."

He looks at me like I'm stupid, but then gives in. "Okay, sure. LibraryDuster1."

I patiently listen to his instructions and then ask a gamer who calls himself Toadface17 to play me. When I'm done losing the game, I look at Pimples and give him half a smile.

Chapter 68

I ALMOST APPRECIATE DARIUS when he keeps me from walking into parked cars a couple of times as I'm fiddling with my GameCom looking for anyone I think might be Conrad. He said he would play the fight me game all day. Is he ConMan22? Or Contraband4?

"Hey, I know you're excited about your new toy, but you really should watch where you're going," Darius says as I almost walk into a car for the third time.

"So, sorry. I'm just trying to figure this game out."

I start playing the fight me game with ConMan22 and type, "I need u to get away from Gr8 at 6:30."

It isn't Conrad. He or she types back. "Nvr playd him im w/Killr Monkys i play @ 6:30 sry." I lose the game against him faster than I did the first one, and as my score shows on the screen, the GameCom tries to get me to play again by saying, "fight me, fight me."

Darius swears at me and points to my GameCom. "If I have to hear 'fight me' one more time today, I'm going to lose it. Can't you play anything else?"

I try to look innocent. "This is the only game I know how to play. Sorry. I'll turn it down."

Suddenly I see a RadOak16 show up as a possible opponent. Where have I seen that before? Conrad's paper! This has to be him. I type to him, "Now is the time. I'm leaving tonight. Slip the thing Ed gave you to Gr8, I'll be at your place at 6:30." I hope against hope that he can figure out that I am LibraryDuster1.

I think he does, because he writes back, "I will do it. Bring something for the lock. Fight me?" I am so happy, I don't even mind losing the stupid game again.

When I get back to school, everyone stares at me like I'm a freak. It must be the GameCom, or Darius. Charlisa sidles up to me as the end of lunch bell rings and whispers, "What is wrong with you? Have you switched sides?"

I cover what I think is the microphone on the GameCom and whisper back, "I had no choice. We're leaving..."

"After school, I know." She slips into her classroom right as the second bell rings.

I wrack my brain for ideas on how to get rid of Darius and the other two patrolmen in the next few hours. Luckily, someone has thought ahead for me. Ed holds up a plate of chocolate cookies as Mr. Moreland, our overweight science teacher gets up from his desk. "Since there aren't very many of us left in here, I thought I'd bring a treat to share. Is that okay?"

Mr. Moreland licks his lips. "Sure, that's fine. I hope you brought enough for Mrs. Graight and Patrolman Darius."

"Oh, I did. Don't worry."

I notice that Ed angles the plate a certain way for all of us to get our cookies, but he angles it completely opposite when he offers Patrolman Darius his cookie. Mrs. Graight gets the last cookie on the plate. I wait patiently through the rest of class to see what will happen, but nothing does. I hope Ed gave the right cookies to the right people. All of a sudden, Mr. Moreland jumps up from his chair and runs for the door. "I knew I shouldn't have had cheese with my beefy patty," he mutters as he runs for the lavatory. The bell rings, and I give Conrad a knowing look as we head out the door. He gives me the slightest wink as I follow him out.

I am losing hope that Ed gave something to Darius until we start playing blast ball for physical exercise class. Ed "accidentally" hits Darius in the head with a blast ball as he sits on the sidelines. His eyes close, he leans his head back against the wall, and doesn't move for the rest of class.

I wave my hand back and forth in front of Darius, but he doesn't move. I can hear him breathing, so he's not dead.

Conrad hurries out the door and heads home with Mrs. Graight on his heels. I hope she doesn't black out on the way there. I lean into Ed and ask, "What did you give them?"

"Sleeping formula for large animals, like moose and... elephants," he answers with a grin. "Now hurry up and get your family out of here before he wakes up."

I wrap my GameCom in my jacket and whisper, "But what about the patrolmen following my sister and my mom?"

He slips two packets into my hand and says quietly, "Put this in a drink and give it to them. It takes about an hour to work."

I practically mouth the words, "So why didn't it work on Mrs. Graight?"

Ed looks confused. "I didn't give her any. You're not honestly expecting to get Conrad out in the next few hours, are you?"

My heart drops. "Oh. Uh, I guess not."

Chapter 69

I PACK UP AND LEAVE THE GYM as fast as I can. Charlisa finds me and links her arm with mine. "Don't leave without me. Let's take the backroads to your house. I don't want my mom to see me."

"Okay. Are you sure you want to do this?"

"Of course, I am," she says as a stray tear leaks down her face and off her chin.

I wrap my jacket tighter around my GameCom and turn to look at her. "If your mom finds us, I just want you to know that a man named Jim Yesterly is building a bridge over the boundary wall. It will be ready in a year."

"Stop acting like I'm not coming through with you right now!" Charlisa says anxiously.

We run out of alleys, so we turn onto a main road right as Adamar and Ed turn onto it from the other side. Charlisa lets go of my arm and links hers with Adamar instead. He kisses her as tears run down her cheeks. "We can do this, Charlisa. Don't look back."

All of a sudden, an old black car cuts us off. Charlisa's mom jumps out and grabs her daughter's arm. "What do you think you're doing, Charlisa? How many times have I told you to stay away from this riffraff?"

"I'm not coming home with you, Mom," she says through her tears.

"Yes, you are," her mom insists as she drags Charlisa to the car.

"No, Mom! I want to go with him!"

"Absolutely not."

I keep waiting for Charlisa to break away from her mom and run for it, but she doesn't. She actually hugs her mom and bawls as she lets her mom push her into the car.

Adamar runs to the door of the car and tries to open it. Charlisa's mom hits him and kicks him like a madwoman until he backs off. Tears stream down his face as he calls, "Charlisa, I'll never forget you!"

She rolls down the window and cries out as her mom drives away, "I'll never forget you either. I'll find you one day.

You'll see." The car speeds off like her mom is afraid we'll jump on top of it. Adamar takes off at a sprint down the road after it. Ed runs after him.

My limbs shake as I speed-walk the rest of the way home by myself. Things just got real. As I run into the house, I wonder if my own boyfriend is still on this side of the wall. I have so little time. Think, Dandra.

The neighbor's dog or something is rustling around in our bushes as I see Everley and her patrolman walking down the street. I search frantically for some kind of drink to serve him. We have no milk, no coffee, no juice, wait—I see a carton of apple juice in the back of the fridge. Where did this come from? I don't have time to care. I dump a packet of sleeping formula into a glass of apple juice and stir it up. I grab a child-sized cup and pour some juice for Everley too.

As they walk in the door, I set the drinks at the table and start buttering the last few slices of bread we have. "You must be ready for an afterschool snack, Everley. Sit down and help yourself."

She looks at me suspiciously and sits at the spot with the child-sized cup. "Where did you get the GameCom?"

"Oh, Zane Chesterton gave it to me for free so I can model it."

"That's weird," she says as she takes a drink. The patrolman sits down at the table in the spot without a cup. I bring three plates with bread and butter and set one in front of him.

He looks at the dry bread and sneers, "No, thank you. But I wouldn't mind something to drink."

I steady my shaky hand as I hand him the cup he thought was for me. He takes it and chugs the whole thing down in a few seconds. I let out the breath I've been holding. Everley suspects something, but she doesn't ask me anything. How do I get her packed before this guy is out? How am I going to get rid of Mom's patrolman in time?

"Everley, remember, Mom said we had to have our rooms clean before she gets home. Let's get that done now."

"Okay," she says, shoving the rest of her bread in her mouth. She follows me obediently up the stairs.

Everley swallows and whispers as we enter her room, "What is going on?"

I wrap my GameCom in a blanket before answering quietly. "I gave that guy some sleeping medicine. Baldwin finished the tunnel while we were at school. We have to get packed and leave before the patrolman wakes up."

"What about Mom?"

"I don't know. I don't think I have enough time to give some to the patrolman with her and wait for it to work. I might just have to...knock him out and tie him up."

"Wow." Everley looks at me and giggles. "I hope this works. I hate that guy."

We each fill our backpacks with some clothes, matches, and a blanket. We quietly walk down the stairs to find water bottles and food in the kitchen when we hear a soft snore. I've never heard a more beautiful sound. Everley gets to work looking for food and water while I pack a bag for Mom.

I plan a violent attack as I pack. Mom and her patrolman will be here in forty-five minutes. When they enter the house, I will knee the patrolman between the legs and then hit him on the head with my dad's old baseball bat. Once he's down, I'll tie him up. I can't believe I'm imagining myself doing this. The scariest thing is—I know I can, and I will.

I sit quietly at the window until I see Mom and her escort at the gate. My nerves are absolutely on edge as I place Everley at the table with the sleeping patrolman in order to distract the third and final patrolman from his forthcoming doom—me. I hide behind the kitchen door with our baseball bat, willing my heart to quiet its pounding.

As the door opens, I rush at the first person who walks through. I have to stop my knee mid-thrust when I realize my mom walked through first. I bring the bat up and hit the tall patrolman on the head, but I'm a second too late and all it does is make him swear and take my bat away like I'm a naughty child. He wraps his hand around my throat and starts to squeeze. I can hear my mom's screams and protests as everything starts to go dark.

Suddenly, everything gets light again. The crushing fingers leave my throat, and I see Baldwin with his elbow wrapped around the patrolman's neck. I watch as my enemy's face turns red, then purple, then he falls to the floor and stops moving.

I jump into Baldwin's arms and hold him like the knight in shining armor that he is. He kisses me then pulls me back. "We have to go, now! Gordon and Marcella are already through; the hole comes out in the backyard of a—I think it's a church. There is some kind of choir practice going on right now, so we're incredibly lucky about that. Unfortunately, when I tried to get ahold of Ernestine last night, she didn't answer. She doesn't think we're coming for another week, so we'll be on our own for a while."

I wonder how nosy churches are in the United Cities. They might find us in their backyard immediately, or they might never notice us back there at all. "How will we survive in an unknown country without Ernestine, Baldwin?"

He smiles. "Believe it or not, this isn't my first time being homeless. We'll be fine. I took as many useful things as I could from the shed through the hole already, and I just got Ed and Adamar through. I guess Charlisa's mom took her away as she was headed here, so Adamar is a mess. But, anyway, we need to go now, before any of these patrolmen wake up, and before the cement truck arrives!"

My mom and sister don't need telling twice. I carry everything I can to the tunnel for my mom, who is bawling and complaining that she didn't get to tell Mark goodbye as we go. Baldwin has ripped several of the boards off the shed door. We can barely fit through. Almost immediately, I feel stupid for complaining. If that was a tight entrance, the hole at the end of the tunnel is at least half that size. I'll have to slither through the five feet of dirt like a snake. Yikes. All of the bags go first, then Everley, then my mom. Baldwin presses my back, and I almost go through. I am this close to freedom, but I'll be leaving Conrad to live the rest of his live as a prisoner for telling the truth....

I can't do it.

I turn to my boyfriend and insist, "Go through without me, Baldwin. I'll be right back."

He grabs my arm. "No. I won't let you. We have to go now!"

I rip his hand off my arm. "I can't leave without him. I'll be back in twenty minutes, I promise."

"There's no way, Dandra! Look at my watch. The cement truck will be here in 20 minutes. Forget about him and save your family."

"Then I'll be back in 18 minutes. He would do the same thing for me. Go! We'll be right behind you."

I run away from him and don't look back. I run all the way to Conrad's house on Oak Street. I try to slow my breathing as I approach the door. Oh, shoot. I think Conrad said that I would need a way to pick the lock.

I think my lateness comes in handy because Conrad is the one who opens the door. Relief washes over me that he got the door unlocked by himself. "I'm so glad to see you, Conrad. We have to run, now! We only have 10 minutes."

I reach for his hand, but a big hand clamps down on Conrad's shoulder and pulls him back in. "You're not going anywhere with her," Zane Chesterton's voice slurs.

"Actually, I am," Conrad says in the most authoritative voice I've ever heard come out of his body.

Zane drains his glass and shatters it on the fancy stone floor. "You can't do anything without my permission, boy. This is the price you pay when you go against me." He hiccups slightly. "No one goes against me." His hand tightens on his son's shoulder.

Conrad does the most amazing move I've ever seen as he takes his Dad's arm, twists it, and flips the drunk man over his back onto the hard entryway floor. I cringe as I see pieces of glass imbedded in his skin. Zane mumbles a few things like, "Knows you're coming. You're always watched. Don't take. Mine, always mine," but he doesn't get up.

I stare at him a second too long. Conrad grabs my arm and pulls me out the door. "He's drunk again. Don't feel sorry for him. Let's get out of here before Mrs. Graight comes out of the lavatory."

"Okay, you're right. That was—amazing. Sorry I'm late."

Conrad's eyes are filled with mixed emotions. "I was beginning to worry that you weren't coming for me."

I feel so ashamed. "I almost didn't, actually. It's been a rough day."

"I believe you."

We run as fast as we can until we see the cement truck parked outside our fence. A super-long trough is sending thick gray concrete into the tunnel. Oh, no.

Chapter 70

I CAN'T BELIEVE IT, I'M TOO LATE. My family and friends are on the other side. Conrad takes my hand, and we walk back to the shed. A few more boards are ripped off, and there is a lot of concrete pouring down the hole.

"You're too late," a familiar voice says from behind us. Darius walks slowly toward us from the edge of the bushes. "What did you do to me? I feel like I'm walking through cement, if you'll pardon the expression."

My mouth is incredibly dry. "Sleeping powder."

He shakes his head. "It was too little, too late. Your mom

and sister may have slipped through already, but I've stopped the two people Zane cares most about, so I win."

I am so disgusted by his words that I think my body starts acting on its own. I grab Conrad's hand and run for the shed. I gasp, "Let's run through the cement and be free. Can you do it?"

Conrad's eyes are filled with dread, but he says, "Yes."

I hurl myself around the cement trough and down the ladder as quickly as I can. My chin gets scraped in the narrow space. I hear Darius screaming and swearing right behind us. Conrad is on my heels. Forget running, this stuff is thick. I start walking through the knee-deep concrete, and immediately regret my decision. There is no light anymore. The cement is the worst texture I have every exposed my skin to. It slows me down by at least ten times my previous speed.

"Conrad, I don't know if we can make it through this."

"We can, Dandra. Keep going. I'm right behind you."

Darius lowers himself until he gets to the concrete. "You are both fools. You'll be stuck down here forever. This is quick-dry cement."

Conrad whispers into my ear, "Don't listen to him. Keep going."

Each step is absolute torture. I feel the skin on my legs and feet starting to burn as I force them in and out of the thick cement. I feel claustrophobic for the first time in here. I worry that I might die in this quickly-filling tunnel. I hear a different voice call my name, "Dandra! Come toward my voice." It's Baldwin.

He will help me. I can do this. I hear Darius calling to the cement worker up top, "Get in there and pull them out!"

I move just a little bit faster. Then I hear Everley and my mom calling, "Dandra, don't slow down. Keep walking. We'll pull you out." I find my second wind and keep marching.

Conrad feels like he's falling behind me. I call behind me, "Conrad, are you all right?"

"Yes. I'm fine. Keep going, Dandra."

I can tell that the cement is above my knees now. I don't know if I can take another step. "I can't move."

I feel hands reaching for me. I scoot a few inches closer to the hands, and somehow, they grab my fingers and pull me up. I feel like my fingers are going to rip off my hands until someone gets a secure hold around my wrist. My body feels long and heavy inching its way out of the hole. I devour the clean air as I collapse on the ground. I can't believe it; I made it!

Everyone hugs me and kisses me and tells me how worried they were, and then I realize that Conrad isn't out. I try to stand up on my burning legs. "Get him out! Now!" I scream. Baldwin's face goes from relief to dismay as he looks at Conrad's arm flapping around in the hole. I grab my boyfriend's hand. "Baldwin, if you love me at all, you'll get him out," I cry as my body starts to shut down. I flop onto the ground.

Baldwin's eyes fill with concern as he yells, "Gordon, Ed, help me get him out."

The three of them pull and pull. Adamar wipes his eyes and joins them, and they pull some more. I come to myself and realize that if Conrad doesn't get out now, his whole body will be encased in cement and stuck in five feet of dirt forever. I jump off the ground and immediately fall over. My legs don't feel so good. I scoot on the ground until I can reach a handful of Conrad's shirt. I pull it with a surge of adrenaline that comes right when I need it. Conrad is panting in agony as he is ripped from his tomb of concrete and dirt. He collapses on the ground and moans. His rescuers collapse on the ground, too.

Conrad's face is almost unrecognizable with so much dirt caked on it. He spits over and over again like he's been poisoned. I wrap my arms around him. "I'm so sorry, Conrad."

He kicks his feet as his skin burns. "Ow. It burns, but it's—I'm just glad you came back for me."

I turn his face to look at me. "Did the cement worker get to you?"

He shakes his head. "No. He got one handful of shirt, but that's all." He points to the missing hem of his shirt. "I think he turned back as soon as he took a few steps in."

Baldwin pulls me away from Conrad and wraps his arms around me. "What were you thinking? You almost died."

"I know. I'm sorry."

"How do your legs feel?"

"Like they're on fire," I cry.

Conrad groans and starts wiping his legs all over the ground. "It's eating my skin."

An unfamiliar, deep female voice says, "You two need a doctor before your skin blisters off. I happen to know a good one. I can take you there."

I look up in the darkening sky to a tall, dark-haired woman.

"Who are you?"

Baldwin answers before the woman can. "She's Ernestine. How did you know we were here?"

She smiles at us and says, "You must be Baldwin. I'm Ernestine. My son heard you trying to contact me last night. He said you were coming through a place where people were singing. I knew this had to be the place. The Church of All-Day Praises has choirs singing from noon until midnight every day. I'm glad I was right. Congratulations, everyone. You've made it to the United Cities. You're free."

About the Author

Heather Hayes loves a good story. She believes a good story will entertain you and leave you feeling like a better person for having read it. She loves living in Idaho with her husband and five daughters. If she isn't writing, she is probably watching a volleyball game, cooking, skiing, reading, or planning a trip to somewhere new.

A Message from Heather Hayes

If you liked immersing yourself in Dandra's world, please tell your friends about it and leave a review on Amazon or Goodreads. It helps me out so much, and I love hearing from my readers.

Find more dystopian books by Heather Hayes on Amazon and HeatherHayesAuthor.com.

The Complex Life

The Complex Law

The Complex Leader

If you like a good story for younger readers, check out my other books:

Unexpected Magic

A Tale of Regrets

Rissy's Summer Son

The Fantastic Backyard of Imagination